Loving Cassie

by

JoMarie DeGioia

PUBLISHED BY:

Bailey Park Publishing

Loving Cassie

Book Three of the
Cypress Corners Series

by

JoMarie DeGioia

Chapter 1

Chapman Financial, Boston

Slap!

Cassie Chapman winced as the slick newspaper slammed down on the polished surface of her father's desk. Bill Chapman wasn't playing. That was for sure. One glance at his red face and furrowed brow told her that.

"Look at this, Cassandra!" her father growled, laying his big hand flat on top of the tabloid.

She peeked at the front page of the paper. There was a lot of skin showing in that picture. And Wally, that doofus, was grinning ear to ear up at the camera.

"What the hell were you thinking?" he asked.

Cassie nibbled on her bottom lip as she searched for some kind of answer to placate him. She'd always been able to play her father like an iPod. Now, though? Now she was up to her neck in her latest mistake and she was damned if she could figure a way out of it.

"He didn't tell me who he was," she said, shrugging her shoulders.

Her father's eyes narrowed. "Or who his father is, I'll bet."

"His father?" Cassie blinked at Bill. "Why does that matter?"

Bill cursed, coming around his desk to pace the length of his spacious office. His relocation gave Cassie an unobstructed view out the wall of windows. Pity the gray April sky didn't do a thing to lift her mood. The thunderclouds following her father around the office didn't help, either.

"His father is the U.S. Ambassador to Denmark, for God's sake!"

"Wally never told me that," she said.

Bill turned to pin her with eyes as bright a blue as hers. "Really? You never got around to talking about just what the guy was doing in Copenhagen?"

Cassie crossed her legs, attempting to look calm even as her stomach was churning. She ran her palms over her Lucky jeans-clad thighs in an effort to soothe herself. She should have known better than to buy the line Wally had given her. He'd said he was the heir to some banking empire in the States with money to burn. He'd wanted to party and she was always up for a party.

"I don't know why any of this matters, Dad. Wally and I met up with a few of his friends. That's all."

"His friends. Friends with highly-placed, high-profile

parents."

"So?"

"Friends with as little sense in their heads as you."

His words singed her but she didn't let it show. "We partied. That's all."

"You're tangled up in this mess, Cassie." Bill blew out a breath and sank back down in his chair. "The ambassador's son has been in and out of rehab over the past year. Just tell me you didn't take anything with him."

Now she was angry. "I don't do drugs, Dad. I never have."

Bill nodded, raking a hand through hair still thick, dark and rich. He looked a lot like her two brothers, Rick and Jake. Tall and broad and handsome. A pang settled in the center of her chest. She missed her brothers. It felt like forever since she'd seen them and she hadn't seen Rick's little boy since he was born four years ago.

"Yeah, yeah," Bill said. "I know."

"That's something," she grumbled.

He glared at her again. "Look, young lady. You're not a kid anymore. God, you remind me of your brother Jake."

Cassie hid her smile. Jake was everything she wished she was. Bold and adventurous even if now he was, of all things, settled.

"Jake has a good life, Dad."

A shadow passed over Bill's face and he turned away. Cassie knew what he was thinking. Neither Rick nor Jake had anything to do with their father now. They were both married and settled and, even though they only exchanged emails, Cassie knew they were happy. That pang moved down to her stomach. Happier than their mother had ever been.

"You have to give this time to blow over," her father said.

Cassie focused on her father now. "Let *what* blow over? A party with the son of an ambassador?"

"He's a drug addict, Cassie. And a lot more trouble than the rest of that Euro-trash you pal around with put together."

Cassie bit her tongue at his dismissal of her crowd of, well they weren't exactly friends, but still.

"I'm not seeing Wally. I didn't even sleep with him."

Bill's flush deepened. "I don't want to hear it." He pointed at the blurry photo plastered across the front page of the paper. "You're naked in that picture. And so is he."

Her eyes scanned the photo. She was nearly naked but none of her important parts was showing. As for Wally? Apparently, he'd decided to take a few selfies after she and her girlfriends had fallen asleep. It did look like she'd been up to more than partying, though. There was no denying that.

"So one paper printed Wally's photo. So what?"

Bill jerked open his bottom desk drawer and pulled out a stack of newspapers. "They're all running the photo, Cassie."

Crap. Tabloids printed in several different languages apparently all decided that the story was big news. Or at least big news this week. Her eyes nearly crossed as they ran over the images spread on Bill's desk. Black and white or glossy full color, they didn't look good.

"This will so blow over, Dad." She waved a hand. "I'll just head to London a little earlier than I'd planned."

"You're not going to London."

"I reserved a flat."

"I cancelled it. You can't afford a flat."

Cassie let out a soft laugh. "Yeah, right."

Bill leaned toward her. "You, Cassandra Chapman, can't afford anything."

Her mouth dropped open. No. It couldn't be. Her stomach tightened. "What are you saying?"

"You're cut off."

Alarm trilled through her. "Cut off?"

Bill nodded, and then ran his fingers through his hair again. "Yes, you're cut off." It seemed like he was making this up as he went along but he seemed very pleased with his latest decision. "My money doesn't seem to matter to your brothers. Maybe you should take a lesson from them."

Cassie stood, wishing for a second that she was as tall and imposing as her brothers and father. At least in her heels she neared five seven.

"I know I screwed up, Dad. I should have kept my guard up. Protected myself."

"Cassie, you've always had some crazy guardian angel watching out for you. Skating out of whatever scrapes you stumbled into. Apparently, that's not the case anymore. You can't have the Chapman money to keep you safe, either."

Panic crawled up her throat. "What am I going to do?"

Bill's face brightened and she pulled back, wary. Uh oh.

"What are you going to do?" he asked. "I'll tell you what you're going to do."

Cassie swallowed. "What?" she asked in a soft voice.

Bill smiled but the expression didn't have a touch of warmth to it. "You're going to Cypress."

She clutched the edge of the desk as a flash of emotion

washed over her. Cypress Corners. That wild place in Central Florida where both her brothers had found themselves. One of Chapman Financial's most successful investments and the bane of Bill's existence. That was reason enough to go down there but the big draw for her was seeing her brothers. It was as if the sun broke through the clouds.

"I can go stay with Rick and Harmony," she said. "Jake and Claire just got married, so they'll want their alone time."

Bill's mouth thinned. Her brothers had little contact with their father, and that included Rick and Harmony's adorable little boy, Nick.

"You can work out the details when you get down there," he grumbled.

She sat back down, relief flooding her. "Cypress Corners. It should be nice and warm down there this time of year. I'll hang out by the lake. Maybe head out to the coast for a few days. It's as good a place as any to regroup."

"Oh, you'll regroup all right."

She stared at her father, the bright, sunlit picture in her mind dimming a little bit. "What do you mean?"

Bill crossed his arms. "You, Cassandra Chapman, are going to get a job."

Her breath froze in her lungs.

A job? *Crap.*

***

Cypress Corners, Florida

Tyler Walsh stretched out on his belly, peering under the climbing structure of the newest section of the adventure trails. It was dark under there despite the bright April sun glaring down. The beam of his flashlight showed the red reflected eye-shine, though. It was a gator, all right. And precisely where he shouldn't be at the moment.

"It's a gator, right?" Jake Chapman, the Recreation Director of Cypress, asked.

The animal turned slightly and fixed its gaze on Ty. "Yep." He showed the light on its snout. Six inches. That meant the gator should measure about six feet long, tip to tail. "A six-footer."

Jake blew out a breath of obvious relief. Ty pulled back and grabbed his snare from where it rested on the ground beside him. Nuisance gators didn't fare well in residential areas, but this one could be relocated right here on property, thanks to the acreage. And with seventy-five percent of Cypress Corners' ten thousand acres devoted to wildlife, finding this guy a new home shouldn't be difficult.

Careful application of snare and pole secured the animal and kept both Ty and Jake safe. Jake helped him lift the secured gator into the bed of Ty's Ford F-150.

"Thanks, man," Jake said. "I'd hate to close this segment of the course."

Ty patted the gator's back, and then took off his gloves. "No problem. This guy will do well over on the east side of the property."

Jake nodded and peered into the truck bed. "Jeez, you're like the alligator whisperer."

Ty followed his gaze, and saw that the animal had closed its eyes. "They're pretty docile. For the most part."

"Yeah." Jake chuckled. "For the most part, I'm happy to keep away from them."

Ty smiled at his friend. "Just give me a call anytime, Jake. It's what I'm here for. And let me know when this part of the course is opened. I want to give it a go."

Jake gave him a grin and a two-fingered salute. "Will do."

Ty got into his truck and made his way toward the east side of Cypress Corners. The property encompassed ten thousand acres of some of the prettiest land in the region. It was unusual that more than half the land was set aside as a sanctuary for native plants and animals, but it made his work a welcome challenge. The rest of it was dedicated to expensive homes, retail stores, and recreational facilities, and he could appreciate the money that generated for the developers and investors. There were times he wished he had a stake in the place, but he had enough on his plate without thinking about building his portfolio.

He stopped his truck among the thick brush ringing one of the many ponds that dotted the wildest part of Cypress and set the brake. The gator wouldn't be difficult to release. Not once he lowered the lift gate and loosened the bonds holding him. With very little encouragement, the animal took the freedom Ty offered and was soon splashing his way into the deep end of the pond.

After watching for a couple of minutes to make sure the gator safely settled in, he got back in the truck and entered the info on his tablet. He had to report the gator and its new location to his boss at the Cypress Corners Institute. He still had to head into town, though. Although the director didn't ask him to, Ty had gotten into the habit of checking in face-to-face before the weekend.

The ride to the Institute, situated in the heart of the town center, wasn't a long one. As he made his way, the scene around him gradually shifted from wild to tame to manicured. The town center itself was very picturesque. Though less than fifteen years old it had the look and feel of an historic downtown in New England. It was pretty, but Ty liked the wild parts of Cypress as much as he did the civilized ones.

He parked the truck in the crushed-shell lined lot set beside the Sales Center and stepped out.

"Hi, Ty," a woman called.

He raised a hand to wave at Tammy from the Sales Center.

She stepped off the porch as he approached. "I hear you wrestled that gator into submission."

Ty deflected the woman's obvious overture. Tammy had been flirting hard and steady since he'd started working at the Institute four months ago. He'd tried really hard to keep things friendly without encouraging anything more. He didn't need the entanglement and one look at her told him she was all about tying a guy in knots.

"No wrestling needed," he said. "Or submission."

She gave a throaty laugh and tilted her head to the side, letting her shining dark hair fall over her shoulder.

He couldn't help giving her a quick up-and-down, though. She was a beautiful woman, if way too polished for his tastes. Still, he figured it didn't hurt to look as he noticed a couple more of her shirt buttons were undone than probably should be.

"Yeah, Jake said you're magic with animals," she said.

Ty brought his gaze back to her flawlessly made up face. "I don't know about magic, Tammy. You just have to know how to handle them."

Her brows arched and he laughed off the innuendo before she made it.

"I have to go check in at the Institute," he said.

His friend Rick Chapman, Jake's brother, stepped out of the Sales Center just then.

"Ty. Just the guy I want to see."

"Yeah? What's up?"

Rick stepped down and approached. "I need you to do me a favor, man. Our sister is landing at OIA in about an hour and we have this thing at the school with Nick. Pre-K parents' night, if you can believe it."

Nick was Rick's little boy, and a cooler kid Ty had never met. As for the sister? He'd only heard about her and not all that much.

"You need me to pick her up?"

"Could you? Jake's tied up with some test run on part of one of his courses."

Ty smiled. "Yeah. Seems an alligator put a crimp in his time frame."

Rick laughed, and then took out his phone and ran his thumb over the screen. "Here. I'll text you her flight info. I'm going to send her your info, too. Just drop her at my house when you get back?"

"Sure thing."

Rick thanked him again as he turned back into the Sales Center. Ty glanced at his phone and read the info Rick sent him. She was due in at five-ten at Orlando International Airport. That wasn't too bad. He'd be able to get her and bring her over to Rick's and get back home by seven the latest.

Pulling up the director's info, he tapped the screen and got the man on the line. He verbally checked in, and then wished the guy a nice weekend and thanked him for the return of the sentiment. Smiling though the director couldn't see it, he ended the quick call and pocketed his phone.

"So what are you up to this weekend?"

He'd forgotten Tammy was standing there. "Family stuff."

Tammy wrinkled her nose. "Ugh. Family. I'm so glad mine lives up north."

Ty just nodded. He couldn't imagine living that far away from his family. He had so little of it left. "Have a good weekend."

He got back into his truck and headed out toward the airport. OIA was just about the closest thing to Cypress, sitting about a half hour or so to the northwest of the property. On a good day, that was. On a Friday afternoon, traffic heading into the airport could be heavy. Today wasn't proving to be the exception.

He pulled into the cell phone lot, glanced down at his phone, and saw he had a message from a number he didn't recognize.

"Must be her."

He swiped at the screen and read that she was waiting at baggage claim. He headed out toward arrivals and drove slowly up the ramp. He didn't know near which door she'd be, so he kept his eyes peeled as he made his slow approach with what felt like everyone else in Orlando. The usual suspects littered the sidewalks, luggage set nearby. Families and business travelers and snowbirds wanting to visit Florida just once more before it got too hot for them. A luggage trolley jammed full of bags and suitcases caught his eye. Then the woman standing beside it did, too.

Whoa. She wore a tight purple T-shirt with some writing on it and a short brown leather jacket. Her skirt showed off an hourglass body and long legs that ended where tan high-heeled sandals wrapped her feet. Long, dark hair was held back from her face by oversized sunglasses and, as he pulled alongside of her, he caught the family resemblance. She had Rick's dark hair and Jake's blue eyes, but she was all woman. And a beautiful one at that.

Lowering the passenger-side window, he leaned toward her. "Are you Rick's sister?"

She stared at him, her rosebud mouth dropping open. "Y-yes."

He grinned at her. "Well, I'm your ride."

Chapter 2

Cassie stared at the gorgeous guy who'd just pulled up to the curb in his big silver truck. When Rick had texted that he couldn't pick her up, she'd been disappointed. Not now, though. The handsome face that smiled at her from the driver's seat made her belly heat.

He got out of the truck and walked around to the curb. He was tall. And broad, judging by the flannel shirt he wore open over his snug T-shirt. And his khakis looked worn and broken in and hung just right off his narrow hips.

"Ty Walsh." He stuck out his hand and she took it.

"Cassie Chapman."

His hand was a little calloused and his grip was firm. "Sorry your family couldn't get you."

"Yeah." Her eyes flicked over him. "Sorry."

What was wrong with her? She'd just spent the past six months with pretty, shiny guys all over Europe, for God's sake. This guy was hot, though. Even if he wasn't her type. Shaggy sun-streaked hair, a dusting of stubble along his jaw. Big hazel eyes. And God, he had dimples.

"Jeez, is all this yours?" he asked.

She blinked, and then focused on the luggage cart. "Yes."

He whistled, and then smiled at her. "I take it you're going to be staying a while."

It wasn't all that many bags. So she'd brought some of her favorite things with her. She'd only packed the essentials, really. But the reality of having everything she cared for stashed and hauled down here to Florida with her? It sucked.

"I've been exiled."

He gave a short laugh, a rumble really, and she felt it tickle over her. She grabbed up her big Jimmy Choo hobo bag and slung it over her shoulder. Ty seemed to have everything in hand, so she just crossed her arms and let him do his thing. She had to admit she liked watching him make quick work of her admittedly large collection of bags.

"I think that's it." He slammed the tailgate up and faced her, running his fingers through that thick, messy hair of his. "Ready?"

She licked her lips and nodded. "Yes."

He opened her door and she climbed in. A rough-around-the-edges gentleman. Hmm. The leather seat was soft against the backs of her thighs as she settled into it. She placed her bag at her feet and buckled herself in as he rounded the front. He slid into the driver seat, buckled, and then shifted to pull them away from the airport.

"So, Ty, is it?" she said.

"Thomas Tyler Walsh the third, actually. But I've been Ty for as long as I can remember."

She just nodded. He was a "the third?" All the other "thirds" she had ever known were spoiled prep-school pretty boys. This "third?" He didn't look spoiled and he wasn't a pretty boy.

It was very close in the truck's cab and she could smell him. He smelled like the outdoors. Fresh and hot. He had some mud caked on his work boots and a quick glance behind his seat showed her a plastic file tote filled with files and folders.

He caught her gaze and shrugged. "This truck is my office."

"What do you do?" she had to know.

"I work for the Cypress Institute."

She brightened. "Oh, like Harmony?"

He threw a smile at her and she sucked in a breath. That smile was potent.

"Sort of," he said. "Her thing is plants, though. I handle animals."

She watched his strong hands as he easily maneuvered through the traffic threatening to clog the exit ramp. His sleeves were rolled up and his arms looked tanned and strong.

"You handle animals."

She had no idea what that could mean.

"I'm the Wildlife Technician on property."

"Nope," she said with a smile. "Still no clue."

He laughed again. "I make sure their habitats are preserved. Secure. That they're safe. And that they don't bother the residents and visitors too much."

A trickle of unease flowed over her. "Just what kind of animals?"

"Alligators, mostly. Some raccoons awake when they shouldn't be. That type of thing."

She sensed something more to his story. Something he was keeping back. "Is that all?"

"All right, you've got me." His dimples made a reappearance. "Snakes and wild boar, too."

She shivered. "Yikes. Just what is this place?"

He glanced over at her, one golden brow arched. "You've never been to Cypress?"

She shook her head and played with the flap on her jacket pocket. "I've been out of the country."

"Yeah. Jake told me you were a globe-trotter."

She just shrugged. She could only imagine what else her

brother had told this guy. Did Jake know about the pictures? Rick had to. Their father had contacted her big brother when everything hit the fan last week. Cold settled in the pit of her stomach.

"No trotting for me now, though." She took a breath and straightened her shoulders. "I'm stuck here in the wilds of Florida for the foreseeable future."

"Ah, it's not so bad."

She eyed his lean, muscled body as he turned the wheel. *Nope. Not so bad.* She fiddled with the air vents and held her hair up off the back of her neck. It was getting hot in here.

"How long have you been in Cypress?" she asked him.

"Going on four months. It's a great opportunity for me. I live right on the property, too."

"I guess I'll see you around the place, then."

His gaze ran over her bare legs and she felt goose bumps break out all over her body. "Sure."

They spoke a little about the weather and not much else until he straightened a bit in his seat.

"Here we are."

She looked to the left as Ty steered the truck into the entrance of Cypress Corners. A long drive bracketed by white ranch fencing and tall leafy trees led them toward what must be the center of town. It didn't look anything like she'd imagined. Not the rough land Ty had described and not even like the few-and-far-between houses she'd seen as they'd driven out of St. Cloud through ranch and farmland. No, this place was quaint and pretty. Like a picture postcard of some small town she'd never visited and only read about.

"This is pretty," she said.

"It is." He slowed as they passed a coffee shop, and then pulled to a stop on the corner. "The Clubhouse is straight ahead. That's the fancy restaurant on property. They have a tavern tucked in there, too. Great burgers."

She just stared at the elegant façade of the Clubhouse. She'd heard her father talk about Cypress and, by the scenic golf course she could see beyond the Clubhouse, this was a very successful project indeed. It was a little weird that it had a folksy town center, though.

"The Sales Center is just behind us, to the left."

"Rick's domain?" she asked.

Ty nodded. "I'm sure he'll show you around. Take you on one of the property tours."

Yeah, her brother could drive her around but she might like

this hot wild animal tamer to do it instead.

"Um, do you give those?" She swallowed. "Tours, I mean?"

He chuckled. "Not the ones for prospective residents, I don't."

"What do you mean?"

"I lead eco-tours. Into the wild, so to speak. Tamed adventure, believe me. But adventure, just the same."

She couldn't help but smile. "You sound like my brother, Jake. He goes on about those courses of his."

"You'll have to give them a go. They're pretty amazing."

She shook her head. "No way, thanks. I'll take hot yoga or maybe a swim, but that's about as sporty as I get."

Ty eyed her legs again, which she admitted didn't look too bad, and then pulled the truck forward.

"We'll see," he said. "Cypress has a way of changing people."

"Not me."

He just shook his head. Did he think she needed to change? He had made that comment about her bags, but so what? She was visiting family, and she had no idea for how long. She wouldn't let this nature guy make her feel bad or that she needed to be different than she was.

She could do that all by herself, thanks.

***

"Rick and Harmony live over near the main lakeshore," Ty said. "I'm sure they're back from the school thing by now."

"With Nick?"

"Yeah. He's a great kid."

"I wouldn't know."

He didn't say anything to that. Her voice sounded a little sad.

"I haven't seen Nick since he was an infant," she explained.

He hadn't expected that. "Then you're in for a good time. That kid is terrific."

She just nodded, her face turned away from him.

He stopped the truck in front of the gorgeous two-story house where Rick and Harmony lived. It was set on a large lot, and had a beautiful view of the central lakeshore across the street. A deep porch stretched across the front of the house, dotted with Adirondack chairs and a hanging bench swing. Columns and a railing enclosed the porch, making it look very inviting.

The house was painted a dove gray and the roof was peaked slate. The large carriage lights on either side of the wide front door were lit. Anyone would find it all very welcoming, but he couldn't shake the feeling that Cassie was a little uneasy.

"Their house is lovely," she said in a small voice.

Ty just made a sound of agreement and shut off the engine. He climbed out and she did likewise. She stared up at Rick and Harmony's house, suddenly very still. Then the front door opened.

"Hey, Cassie."

They both looked up at the front door, where Rick now stood with a big smile on his face.

"Hi, Rick," Cassie said.

Rick stepped down, slowly coming closer to them on the walk. He looked as uncertain as Cassie did for that brief moment, and then he smiled again.

"I've missed you, sis."

Cassie blinked her long lashes and Ty could tell she and Rick were both getting choked up. He had to get out of there and fast. This was a family thing and, from what little she'd said about it, she hadn't been around this family much.

"Cassie!" Jake shouted as he barreled out of the house and down the steps to wrap his sister in a bear hug. "God, it's been too long."

Apparently this Chapman didn't have trouble with the love stuff. After a slight hesitation, Cassie returned the hug and buried her face in Jake's neck. Rick placed a hand on her shoulder and one glance up at the open front door showed that both Harmony and Jake's wife Claire held back to give the siblings their time. He shared a small smile with each of them and stepped back.

"Ty, come in and join us for dinner?" Harmony asked.

Ty shook his head. "Thanks, but I'll leave you guys to your reunion." He walked back to the truck. "Besides, I have to get home."

Rick took in a deep breath, and then nodded to Ty. "Thanks for getting her here safe and sound, man." He walked to the back of Ty's truck. "Give Jake and me a few minutes to handle her mountain of stuff and you can get out of here."

Ty dropped the lift gate and reached for the first piece of luggage. Jake finally released Cassie and came over to wave him away. Ty just laughed off the attempt and the three men made quick work of her bags, carrying them into the house to pile them in the marble-tiled foyer. When he closed the lift gate, he found her standing close to him. They were alone for the moment.

"Thank you, Ty."

He looked down at her and smiled. "No problem, Cassie."

She looked much smaller to him now, especially after hugging her brothers. He would guess, without her heels, she'd be about the same height as Harmony. Five three or four, maybe. He noticed that hesitancy was back again, too.

"I'll see you around?" she asked.

It was a question he had no problem answering. "More than likely."

She flashed him a smile, it was bright and genuine, and he felt a kick to his gut.

"Aunt Cassie?" a little voice called from the porch.

If he hadn't been watching her so closely he would have missed her stiffen at Nick's call.

"Yep." She turned to face the house again. "That's me."

"Come in, Aunt Cassie." Nick's little face was all lit up as he leaned out of the doorway. "We have pizza!"

Ty chuckled and left the Chapmans to their pizza and their reunion. As he drove to his house, located in one of the more densely populated villages in the property, he breathed in Cassie's scent. It lingered in the truck's cab. Something flowery, maybe. Sweet, too. Like one of those sugar-dusted flowers he'd seen in the bake case at the coffee shop.

Man she was hot, though. He'd more than noticed that on the drive back from the airport. That body of hers, with that short skirt inched up her smooth thighs on his truck seat. Those gorgeous blue eyes that caught his gaze a couple of times. Those lips that were still full and ripe even when she was frowning.

She was a contradiction. That was for sure. Tough as nails and a little cold and then a tender marshmallow when her big brothers hugged her. Yeah, she was a contradiction all right. And a complication he didn't need right now.

As he pulled into his driveway, he gave his house the once-over. It was smaller than Rick and Harmony's, but just as nice. Quaint front porch set with a couple of chairs. Clapboard siding and deep eaves. All the houses in Cypress looked very traditional but he knew they were state-of-the-art at their guts. Wired for just about everything and supremely comfortable. It was his house but he spent just as many nights out on the far lakeshore. Sometimes he just needed to sleep under the stars.

He stepped through the door from the garage and greeted his mother standing in the kitchen. Sharon Walsh was a pretty woman, in her mid-fifties but wearing it well. Her hair was wavy like his but the hazel eyes she'd passed on to him looked tired tonight.

"Hello, Tyler."

Studying her, he weighed the evidence. Today hadn't been too bad, apparently. Tonight he didn't see the telltale crinkles from pain around those eyes so much like his. She looked neat and comfortable in her black yoga pants and pink knit shirt.

"Hi, Mom." He bent down to kiss her offered cheek. "Good day?"

"Very." She reached into the oven and pulled out a casserole. "I went into the town center and talked with Lettie this afternoon. Stopped in the market and even had the energy to make baked ziti."

Ty breathed in the scents of tomato sauce and baked cheese and grinned. "Smells fantastic." He watched her as she placed the dish in the center of the farmhouse table and sat down. He caught it then. The slight wince.

"Are you feeling okay, Mom?"

She waved a hand. "I'm just a little tired, Ty. But I feel good. I promise."

His mother had been fighting fibromyalgia for the last few years, and had her good days and bad. Today, apparently, had been one of the good ones.

He washed his hands, and then grabbed the pitcher of iced tea from the fridge and poured them each a glass. "So how is Lettie?"

His mother laughed and he smiled to hear the sound.

"She's a pistol, that one! You know, she takes credit for every hook-up in Cypress."

Ty almost choked on his iced tea. "Hook-up?"

"Oh, you know. She likes to say she sees connections between couples even before they do." She served them each a portion of baked ziti, his much larger than hers. "Like Rick and Harmony Chapman?"

"Maybe." He dug into his pasta, and then shrugged. "They were together way before we moved here, though."

"Jake and Claire, then. I hear they got together right before Christmas. Did you see any sparks?"

"Sparks? Nope. I'd only just started at the Institute. How was I supposed to see sparks?"

"Oh, I don't know. Lettie says electricity was practically arcing across the town center every time they came close to each other."

Ty couldn't say anything to that. He'd sure felt something in the truck cab with pretty Cassie Chapman, though. And a pull out there on the sidewalk. But sparks? He doubted any such thing existed.

"Did you hear from Hank?" he asked her.

His mother frowned at the mention of Ty's sister's ex. "He called. Said you could pick Riley up tomorrow at ten. No later, apparently. He's going to a gun show up in Orlando."

Ty bit back a curse, and then nodded. "Did he say how long we can keep her?"

His mother picked up her glass and he knew she was stalling.

"Mom, what did Hank say?"

She put down her glass and sighed. "He said to bring her back by three."

"By three? That's all we get to see her this weekend?"

"He's her father, Ty. Your sister hadn't expected…" She sniffed. "She made no provisions. No will. He's her father and that's that."

"I want more than 'that's that' for my niece. I want to be able to see her anytime we want to."

"So do I."

He could see the color rising in her cheeks and dropped the subject before she got more upset. His mind worked as he ate, though. Riley was only three years old. She was all they had left of his reckless sister and he loved her as if she were his own.

He thought of the family reunion he'd witnessed tonight. Of the separation the Chapmans had withstood over the past few years. That kind of estrangement wasn't what he wanted for Riley. He'd figure out how to get their little girl a permanent place in their lives.

Problem was, he was damned if he knew how to do it.

Chapter 3

Cassie sat on a stool at the raised granite counter in Rick and Harmony's house the next morning, nursing her cup of coffee. She still wore what she considered her pajamas, just a pair of Juicy sweatpants with a T-shirt. She rubbed her hands over her face as she stifled another yawn. The sun was barely up but she couldn't stay in bed a minute longer.

She hadn't slept much last night, and for the first time in a long time she couldn't blame it on partying too hard or drinking too much. No, she'd barely eaten the pizza and hadn't drunk more than a sip of the beer Jake grabbed her from the huge stainless fridge. They'd all tried to include her in their conversations but she'd still felt so out of place.

Her brothers' wives were wonderful. Sweet, welcoming, and each of them just perfect for her very different brothers. Harmony brought out a warmth in Rick that Cassie couldn't remember seeing since before their mom died over sixteen years ago. And Claire was just the woman to keep her daredevil brother Jake's feet on the ground. Cassie briefly wondered when they would add a little one to the family gatherings. If the kisses, cuddles, and steamy looks they exchanged were any clue, it wouldn't be very long. The thought of another Chapman baby felt bittersweet to Cassie.

Not that she didn't like Nick. She did. He was a terrific kid, just like Ty Walsh had said. She had no clue how to act around him, though. Her circle of whatever they were, she couldn't think of the people she'd hung around with as friends, had no leanings toward having children. None of them did commitment, and starting a family called for a massive dose of commitment.

She placed her empty cup in the sink and looked around the large, open kitchen and the spacious great room. She hadn't really known what she'd expected but, after seeing the beautiful exterior and landscaping outside, the interior didn't disappoint. It was large, bright and furnished with obvious care. Harmony made a wonderful home for Rick and their son. It was warm and comfortable and left a hollow feeling in the pit of Cassie's stomach. She didn't belong here.

As much as she loved her brothers, and she'd missed them even more than she'd thought, she felt like an intruder on their domestic bliss. She swallowed past the lump in her throat. She felt like a phony.

"Hey, you're up early," Harmony said as she walked into the kitchen.

Cassie smiled at her sister-in-law. Harmony looked so pretty and fresh, even this early in the morning. She wore sherbet-striped pajama pants and a soft-looking long-sleeve shirt in a light green. Her honey-colored curly hair was pulled up and off her face and her hazel eyes were bright. Their color reminded her of Ty's friendly gaze, and Cassie shoved that thought aside. She couldn't entertain the attraction she'd felt instantly toward him. Nope.

"Good morning." Cassie leaned back against the counter. "Your house is just lovely, Harmony."

"Thanks." Harmony held up a hand. "And before you even start, you're welcome to stay as long as you like."

Cassie laughed softly. "Expecting my defection already? What, am I a flight risk?"

Harmony smiled. "No, but Jake was staying with us and he headed out to the tent-cabin almost as soon as he got here last fall."

"Tent-cabin?"

Harmony put in a coffee pod and started her own cup of coffee brewing, and then faced her again. "I used to live on the far lakeshore before I married your brother. I loved it, but it was a little rustic for Rick."

Cassie laughed. "Yeah, I can't picture my big brother

roughing it."

Harmony got a faraway look in her eyes and Cassie guessed she was thinking about the times they'd shared out there in her tent-cabin, whatever that was.

"That part of the lake was originally going to be developed and it might be someday but right now it's still pretty wild out there."

"Don't you miss it?"

"Oh, I get enough of a nature fix with my job."

"Plants."

Harmony nodded and grabbed up her cup of coffee. "Yep."

Cassie couldn't imagine making any part of nature a career choice, but who was she to judge? She had no career choice to speak of herself. "Ty mentioned it," she said.

She'd thought once more about the guy, darn it.

"Again, I'm sorry we couldn't get you last night," Harmony said. "I'm so glad Ty was able to pick you up."

Cassie thought about being closed up with Ty in his truck. The fresh scent of him. The easy strength of his hands on the wheel. She couldn't think about the hot wild animal tamer as anything more than her brothers' buddy, though. He really wasn't her type and she knew in her soul she sure wasn't his.

"He seems like a nice guy," Cassie said.

Harmony's eyes narrowed a bit as she tilted her head to the side. Just what was she thinking about? Cassie saw a glint come into her gaze and worried that the woman had matchmaking on her mind.

"Ty lives in one of the villages here in Cypress, you know."

Cassie put on the mask of cool disinterest she'd perfected over the years. "Yes. He told me."

Harmony toyed with her coffee cup, looking down into the brew. "He spends a lot of time out at the tent-cabin, though."

That surprised her, but maybe it shouldn't have. "Your place?"

Harmony looked up and smiled. Apparently Cassie's feigned disinterest wasn't fooling her sister-in-law. "He likes to rough it a little."

Cassie felt a tingle go through her. Ty would look amazing out there in the woods, with the lake at his back. Maybe with his shirt off as he chopped wood or fished or whatever he did out there. Rough, all right. And so hot the thought was making her breathe fast.

"Oh," was all she could say.

She didn't miss Harmony's chuckle and had to smile. Oh,

Harmony wasn't an innocent was she? She knew just what she was doing, talking about Ty.

"Want another cup?" Harmony asked, turning back to the coffee maker.

"Maybe, yeah. Thanks." Cassie took in a deep breath, and then blew it out. "So I was almost afraid to ask you this last night. Did Rick tell you why I was exiled down here?"

"Exiled? Ha!" She faced Cassie again. "You sound like your brother did when he was first stranded down here over four years ago."

"He seems very happy here."

Harmony blushed a little as she handed Cassie another cup of coffee. "We both are."

Cassie took the cup and took her time, adding creamer and a little sweetener. She knew Harmony was watching her and letting her decide what to say about the circumstances that brought her down to Cypress. "So, did Rick tell you?"

Harmony nodded. "I didn't see the pictures and I don't care to. I just want to say that you're Rick's sister and mine now, too. We're happy you're here."

Cassie's throat grew tight so she took a long sip of her coffee. Harmony's simple, earnest declaration made Cassie feel welcome and, well, loved. She set the cup down, and then placed her hands flat on the cool granite counter. "Thank you."

It wasn't much but it was from the heart. She'd figure out a way to show her appreciation and soon. First things first, however.

"So, Harmony. Do you know where I can find a job?"

Harmony's brows shot up in surprise. Then, she grinned.

Cassie couldn't help but wonder just what her sister-in-law was thinking. Oh, well. In for a penny.

She only hoped she wouldn't fail at whatever job Harmony had in mind. She couldn't bear to disappoint her family.

Not again.

***

By Monday morning Ty's stomach still churned with frustration. It was always the same for him after bringing Riley back to her father's place. He never exchanged a word with his sister's ex or the guy's wife. Hank was an older guy. Much older than his sister Tracy had been when they'd had their affair. With kids grown up and out of the house. Riley always looked a little sad to say goodbye to her uncle, but Ty tried his best to keep things light. Even now he could feel the warmth of her little arms wrapped around his neck and it made him miss her all over again.

"And the son-of-a-bitch will probably make us wait another week to see her again."

Ty's mother had been visibly tired after their too-short visit with the little girl, but the joy on her face made him bite his tongue regarding Hank and his monopolization of Riley's life.

Tracy's relationship with the guy had been based on the fact that he partied with the kids in town and could always help them score. Tracy had partied hard, too. In fact, ever since she'd hit her teens she never said no to a drink or a hit. The only exception was when she'd been pregnant with Riley. She'd cleaned up her act and straightened out, with Ty and their mom giving her all the support she'd needed. But just weeks after Riley was born it was back to partying like she didn't have a sweet little baby at home probably wondering where her mommy was.

Ty slammed the heel of his hand against the steering wheel. That was the hardest thing of all. They'd given Riley a stable home and it was only after Tracy died in a one-car drunk-driving accident that Hank decided he wanted his daughter to live with him. And Tracy hadn't made any provisions for her baby girl. Ty's mother was right about that. They'd had to hand her over.

That was just two years ago.

As he drove toward the Institute, he thought about blowing off some steam after work today. He needed the workout. That was for sure. Hell, what he really needed was to plant his fist in Hank's face but what good would that do?

Maybe he'd have a go at Jake Chapman's adventure courses later. He could use the distraction of focusing on the obstacles and testing himself, followed by the exertion of pounding his feet over the sandy path as he made his way through the running course. He parked the truck into the lot next to the Sales Center and pulled the brake. Maybe he'd take a swim, too. He smiled to himself. Maybe after a close examination to make sure he didn't run into any buddies of the gator he'd relocated Friday.

Friday. That made him think about Cassie Chapman again. She'd appeared so gorgeous and unapproachable when he'd picked her up at the airport. So hot he'd had trouble thinking about anything else but her legs on their drive back. And all the rest of her. And yet? He guessed there was more to her than her smoking body and ridiculous amount of luggage. Especially after seeing her awkward reunion with her brothers.

He shook his head. Focus, man. Between taking care of his mother and trying to get more than a couple of hours with his niece, he didn't have time to entertain thoughts of getting under Cassie Chapman's tiny little skirt.

He crossed the street and headed toward the Institute. As he turned up the path, he took in the building and its surroundings. Done in soft greens and browns, it reflected the colors of the natural landscape of the place. The edges of the building were softened with plantings exploding with colors. Blues, pinks, and yellows dotted tall fringes of tan and purple grasses. He opened one of the wide glass doors and stepped inside.

Decorated in the colors of true Florida—rich greens, soft tans, and clear blues—the reception area was filled with handmade rattan furniture and breathtaking photos of some of the native plants and animals hung on the textured walls.

He raised his head to say hello to Becky, the receptionist, and froze. The big blue eyes staring back at him made him catch his breath. *Damn.* So much for putting Cassie out of his mind.

"Good morning." He stepped up and leaned his elbows on the counter. "Where's Becky?"

Cassie gave him a wry smile. "Harmony said Becky had to go up to Tallahassee or Cucamunga or someplace in north Florida. Something about a visiting professor."

"So you're working here?"

She shrugged and ran her hands over her hair. It was pulled back in a ponytail and the style made her look fresh and hot at the same time. She wore some kind of silky-looking shirt that hugged her breasts just right and a skirt that rode up a little on her thighs.

"Did you need something, Ty?"

He dragged his eyes back up to her face, his face a little flushed. Jeez, it was like he was sixteen again.

"Uh, I'm just checking in with the director. He in?"

"Yes." She turned to the computer, a look of confusion on her face. "Harmony showed me how to send him a message, but darn if I remember how."

Ty smiled. "Never mind. I'll just go down to his office and knock on his door." He winked. "Old school."

The smile of thanks she gave him made him think about what he'd like to do to earn more of them. Maybe take her out to the tent-cabin and have her smile, and scream, her appreciation to the trees.

His pants felt a little tight and he cleared his throat. "Okay, I guess I'll see you later."

She bit her lower lip and nodded, her brow still furrowed as she studied the computer. Damn, she was adorable. "Sure."

He walked down toward Dr. Robbins' office. The plaque beside the doorframe declared the room to be the director's office, and Ty rapped on the opened door.

"Good morning, Dr. Robbins," he said.

"Good morning."

The director gazed down at his desk as he shuffled at the papers scattered on it. His glasses sat on his balding head as he nodded agreement at something he read. Ty waited a beat, and then cleared his throat. The other man's head shot up.

"Oh!" Dr. Robbins smiled. "Good morning, Ty. Are you set for your tours today?"

Ty smiled back. The director had been welcoming from the very first interview, and Ty loved working for him. The guy seemed absent-minded but Ty knew his mind never stopped working. His skin was tan and Ty knew it was because he spent time outdoors hiking and biking in addition to spending his time behind a desk. He gave Ty the freedom to write his own schedule regarding the eco-tours of the property, and sought out his knowledge for everything from writing grants to handouts for the residents and visitors. As a result, Ty felt valued and very fortunate.

"I have three tours scheduled today," Ty said. "Two on the

west side of the property through the tame trails and one out to the east."

"And who are you touring?"

"The first two are from the high school. One is a group of special-ed kids and the other is the Four-H club." Ty slid the director a smile. "I'm taking some investors out on the tour to the east."

Dr. Robbins grinned. "Ah, that should wrinkle their starch a little bit."

"Yeah. Just think how civilized the village will look when they get back."

The director gave a soft laugh. "Have at them, Ty."

Ty nodded. "I'll be back to check in after each tour."

The director's brows raised. "Oh? You're not going to just text me?"

"Hmm?"

"Could your diligence have anything to do with our new receptionist?"

"What?"

Dr. Robbins didn't buy Ty's innocence, apparently. He just arched a salt-and-pepper brow.

"Um, Cassie is my good friends' sister," Ty said. "How long

is she going to be working here?"

Dr. Robbins just gave him an even look. "Until Becky gets back. A couple of days."

Ty was happy to hear that, but he wasn't going to explore the reason why. It was no mystery, really. Hell, who wouldn't want to see such a pretty picture every time he walked into the Institute's lobby?

The girl looked up to her neck in trouble as he neared the receptionist's desk again. The phone was lit up and she was scrambling as she searched high and low for something. Ty soon guessed what. He could see the up-ended penholder on the floor in front of the desk.

"No, Harmony is out in the property," Cassie said, her voice going high. "I can take a message, though. I think."

Ty grabbed a pen from the floor and handed it to her. She shot him a glance full of appreciation as she cradled the phone against her shoulder and wrote out the message.

"Th-thank you." She hung up the phone and sank back in Becky's chair. "Oh my God, I suck at this."

Ty leaned on the desk as he had earlier. "It'll get easier."

She blew her hair out of her face and smirked. "Yeah? I've never done this before. Heck, I've never had a job before."

Ty laughed. "Right."

"I'm serious."

Ty studied her for a second. She was adorably disheveled and completely in the weeds. She'd never had a job before? He'd been working since he'd turned sixteen. Then again, her father was Bill Chapman. He'd seen the guy when he would visit Cypress with his own potential investors in tow. The guy had "money bags" written all over him.

Cassie was on her knees now, scrambling to pick up the papers she'd dropped. He started to gather up the pens and holder when she came around the desk to do the same. Their hands touched and he felt a spark shoot up his arm. Lifting his head, he found himself face to face with her. Up close and personal. Her lips parted, she had delicious-looking lips, and her eyes were opened wide. He wouldn't let his eyes wander down the front of her shirt again. He wouldn't. Okay, maybe just a peek. Damn, he could see she was wearing a pink bra. With lace. And little bows.

He scrambled to his feet, his pulse racing. "Okay, I better get going."

She licked her lips as she stared up at him, and then nodded. "Thanks for your help."

He muttered something, he wasn't sure what, and helped her to her feet. At this second touch, he felt a punch to his gut.

He managed to say something, something lame probably, and got the hell out of there. He could feel her watching him and suddenly all his clothes felt too tight. Thank God his mother's friend Lettie hadn't seen that little exchange. Lord knew what she'd make of his fumbling and ogling. More sparks talk, he was sure.

The girl never had a job before. They were so different, from their upbringing to their responsibilities. It was a shame, really.

It made him feel so far apart from her right at the moment when he wanted to get much closer.

Chapter 4

By the end of the day, Cassie was ready to scream. Or cry. Or run screaming back to Boston to fall at her father's feet.

"No stinkin' way am I about to do that," she murmured.

"What's that, dear?"

She glanced over to see Dr. Robbins standing at the desk. She knew she had to look like a complete mess. Her hair was falling in her face and her clothes were wrinkled. She'd chewed off her lip-gloss at some point before lunch and never bothered to put it back on. The director didn't seem to notice that, though. Nope, he wore that absent-minded professor thing he'd had going on all day. He didn't glance down the front of her shirt as Ty had, either.

She thought about her little exchange with the hot animal-tamer and her breath came fast. He'd stopped back in a few times during the day, too. She had no idea what he did out in the field but he sure filled out his khakis and Henley quite nicely. Filled the wide doorway when he'd arrived that morning, too.

His hazel eyes fastened to the front of her made her want his big, capable hands to follow. Shaking her head, she focused on the director.

"N-nothing, Dr. Robbins." She stacked the mess of papers

on the desk and smiled. "Did you need something?"

"I was dinging your computer but you didn't answer."

"I, um." She shrugged. "I don't have the knack of that, I'm afraid."

He smiled in a show of indulgence that somehow didn't feel condescending. "You'll come along."

She blew the hair off her forehead for the hundredth time that day. "That's what Harmony says."

The director's brow furrowed. "Becky should be back the day after tomorrow. Can you hold on until then?"

She blinked, and then jumped to her feet. "Of course! I don't want to leave you high and dry."

He reached out and patted her shoulder. "I appreciate that. And it's only one more day, Cassie. How much damage can you do in that time?"

She suddenly wanted to cry. "Hopefully not too much?"

"Go on home, dear." His eyes went the mess on the desk. "You can clean that up tomorrow."

Cassie nodded. "Thank you, Dr. Robbins."

She gathered up her bag from the bottom desk drawer and got the heck out of there. As she walked out of the Institute, blinking up at the bright late afternoon sun, she thought about her confession to Ty that morning.

Admitting she'd never had a job in her life had surprised her. It had apparently shocked him. That was for sure. What did he think about that? That she was lazy? That she was a pampered princess? That she was clueless about the way to actually make your way in the world? Deep in her gut, she suspected at least a couple of those might be true.

"You must be Cassie Chapman," a silky voice drawled.

Cassie turned to see an older woman waving madly at her from the courtyard of the coffee shop. She was seated under the shade of a sprawling flowering tree, a tall glass of sweet tea held in her other hand.

Cassie made her way over the walk to stop at the wrought iron fence bracketing the courtyard. "Hello."

The older woman smiled. "Well, well. Aren't you just the picture of a Chapman."

"What?"

"Forgive me, sweetheart. My name is Charlotte Fairfax, but everyone calls me Lettie. Have since I was a little girl."

"It's very nice to meet you, Lettie."

Cassie found herself smiling at the woman. She wore a large straw hat that Cassie had only seen on women in the movies, her bangs a silvery fringe beneath. A flower-print smock, denim overalls, and a pair of bright green Crocs completed her outfit.

"I was just saying that you're as pretty as your brothers, Cassie. Of a decidedly more feminine bend, of course. And look at that figure!"

Cassie flushed but she couldn't find a drop of irritation in the face of such an outrageous yet apparently sweet person.

"You know my brothers, then?"

Lettie winked. "Not as well as their wives, I'd bet."

Cassie laughed. "No?"

"Oh, if only I was thirty years younger!"

Cassie guessed she was in her seventies but she certainly looked closer to fifty.

"Thirty? Surely not that many."

Lettie chuckled. "Yes indeed, but aren't you sweet. I claim my youthful glow to healthy living, big hats and the liberal application of sunscreen."

"I'll keep that in mind."

"I hear that gorgeous Ty Walsh picked you up?"

Cassie's cheeks heated. "Um, yes. From the airport, yes."

Lettie's blue eyes narrowed. "Do I see sparks?"

Cassie waved a hand. "No, no. Ty is friends with my

brothers. That's all."

"Mmm, mighty fine is that Ty. Reminds me of my dear, late Mr. Fairfax. Mr. Fairfax had dimples, too. Very Clark Gable as Rhett Butler, if you get me." Lettie winked again. "Ty's mother is a good friend of mine. If you were wondering how I knew about his little act of chivalry."

Cassie guessed this particular southern belle didn't miss a thing that happened in Cypress Corners. She would just have to make sure that she kept out of the gossip mill while she was down here. One scandal, okay a few scandals, in her past were more than enough for one lifetime.

"I wasn't. Not really."

"So what brings you down here, Cassie? I couldn't get it out of your brothers. Or their wives. Close as a northern clam, every one of them."

Cassie was grateful for her family's discretion. More than she could ever say.

"I just needed a change of scenery. That's all."

Lettie studied her, and then shrugged. "I'm here most days. Feel free to join me under my favorite tree if you ever want to talk."

Cassie nodded. "I will, Lettie. It was a pleasure meeting

you."

Lettie lifted her glass of tea in salute. "Have a nice night, dear."

As she walked toward the Sales Center to see her brother Rick, Cassie thought about sweet, intrusive Lettie Fairfax. While the woman was nothing like their sad and quiet mother had been, Cassie had felt a wave of affection from Lettie that she hadn't encountered since her mother passed away when Cassie was nine years old. More than sixteen years had passed since their mother died. She'd been without a woman's influence for so long she'd forgotten how warm and close that relationship could be.

As for the friends she'd partied with, she'd always kept them at arms' length. It was what they all did, really. Keep emotion out of it and then no drama would follow. Drama. Those darn pictures were drama enough and, if she was being honest, she'd brought that drama on herself.

Maybe while she was down here in Cypress she could have that closeness she'd missed with her sisters-in-law. They were both friendly and welcoming, and Cassie couldn't wish for better women for her brothers.

She was at a loss at where to go now that her workday, such

as it was, was done. She was a little hungry, but she had no idea about where to eat here except for the pricey Clubhouse. She was pretty sure it wasn't her scene, given that it was one of her father's pet projects and favorite spots. It was probably stuffy and filled with men in golf pants.

"Hey, sis." Jake loped toward her from the direction of the Sales Center. "Here to see Rick?"

"I was just going to check in. See if I could bum a ride to his house. I'm all finished with work."

Jake tilted his head to the side. "You don't sound like it was a very good day."

"Oh, the director is very nice and the work isn't hard. I just don't have a clue."

Jake grinned. "How much damage could you do in a couple of days, right?"

"That's just what Dr. Robbins said."

"Smart man. What are you doing for dinner?"

Her stomach rumbled and she shrugged. "I have no idea. What's good?"

"How about joining me for a burger at the tavern? Claire is heading into St. Cloud to see her dad tonight. It's bingo night so she'd taking him to the mall."

That was puzzling. "What?"

Jake shook his head. "Long story, but suffice it to say the guy isn't allowed to gamble. Ever."

She'd just bet there was a story there but Cassie was no Lettie. She wouldn't pry.

"A burger sounds good."

Jake put his arm around her shoulders. "Then let's go. Ty's waiting in the bar."

She skidded to a stop, her stomach dropping to her toes. "Ty will be there?"

"Yeah." Jake faced her. "We get together a couple of times a week. Why?"

How could she tell her brother that she and Ty had a moment earlier today? Okay, a couple of moments. That strong body. Those warm, hazel eyes. Those dimples. Lettie was right. The man was fine.

"It's nothing." She waved a hand. "I like Ty."

Jake chuckled and they started walking again.

"You like him, huh?"

She nudged him with her shoulder. "Don't start. I got an earful from Lettie Fairfax this afternoon, thanks."

"Lettie speaks her mind, sis. She also never misses a trick."

Cassie didn't say anything more about Ty or Lettie or tricks. She was going to hit the ladies' room before heading into the tavern, though.

A girl should spruce herself up when she was meeting her brother's friend for dinner, right?

***

Ty ran his fingers over the beer bottle, catching the condensation on the label. He'd checked on his mother after work and she seemed to be doing pretty well today. He was thinking about staying out at the tent-cabin tonight. It would make his morning a little bit easier to take. He had a few tours scheduled for tomorrow and Rick wanted him to pop into the Sales Center to speak to a group of potential sales associates he was considering bringing on. Ty was up for anything to promote the development. Cypress was his home now.

He'd grown up in St. Cloud, and he never forgave himself for heading up to Gainesville for college despite the degree that gave him his living today. He'd left his sister Tracy to her own devices. Partly as a defense mechanism, though. Their father was the only one she'd ever listened to and she flat-out rejected everything Ty ever suggested.

The redneck teens she'd hung around with in high school

had grown up to be hard-drinking bullies. She'd gone from one abusive relationship to another before falling in with Hank. She must have been drawn to him because he was older. Their father died while Ty was in University of Florida earning his undergrad. Lung cancer that came as a shock since the man never smoked a cigarette in his life. Tracy had been only fourteen.

He took one last drag on his beer and drained the bottle. He hadn't given himself the luxury of thinking about that dark time in a while. Why the hell he was tonight, he couldn't guess.

"Hey, man."

Ty turned his head to smile in Jake's direction. "Hey."

Jake settled on the stool beside him. "Good Monday?"

"Pretty good."

"How's your mom doing?"

Jake knew his mother had her good days and bad. Ty had confided in him one night over beers right here in the tavern, actually. He never shared the reality of Tracy's death and the mess she'd left behind, though. Just that they watched her little girl occasionally. It was a sore subject for him, since he felt like such a failure every time he had to take Riley back to her father's place.

"She's pretty good, thanks," Ty said. "Feeling stronger. Lately, anyway."

Jake raised a hand to the bartender to order a beer, and then nodded. "That's good. We have a guest joining us tonight, if that's okay."

Ty was pretty easy-going, so he just shrugged. "Sure. Who's—?"

His breath caught as he saw Cassie walking toward them. *Whoa.* She'd let her hair down from her ponytail and brushed it, apparently. Her dark waves fell over her shoulders and a couple more shirt buttons were undone than when he'd seen her last. On Tammy, such a look might have appeared calculated but on Cassie she just looked fresh and natural, with a glow in her cheeks and her lips a glossy pink.

"Cassie, over here," Jake called.

She smiled and Ty felt that earlier punch to the gut move downward. He shifted on his stool. It wouldn't do to sport wood with the girl's brother sitting next to him.

"Hey, Ty," she said.

Her voice was a little husky and it scratched over him in the best way. "Hey."

Jake looked between the two of them when they both grew

quiet, and then smiled crookedly. "Riveting. Let's go eat."

Ty eyed his friend. Jake seemed to sense something but he wasn't one to pry. He knew that from the first time the guys met and that impression had only grown in the months since.

"I'm starving," Ty said.

"Me, too," Cassie put in.

Jake grabbed his beer bottle and took the lead as they headed for one of the round tables dotting the interior of the tavern. The place was decorated much like an English pub, which should have felt strange but it worked given the stuffy pretention available over in the Clubhouse. It was a nice counterpoint.

As they neared a table set near the fireplace that dominated one wall, Ty pulled out a chair for her. Cassie looked at him in surprise, and then dipped her head with a smile. Jeez, what kind of jackasses had she been dating if she didn't expect a guy to hold out her chair?

Jake just shot him an even look and Ty quickly took his own seat. A server appeared and brought them glasses of water. Ty ordered another beer and Cassie asked for a glass of pinot.

After the server left, Jake grabbed the menus set in a holder on the table.

"The burgers are great here," Jake said. "I assume you eat meat, sis?"

Cassie nodded. "Yes, and I'm starving."

Ty couldn't seem to think of a damn thing to say as she sipped at her water. She licked her luscious lips and his mouth suddenly went dry. Covering his reaction, he drank some of his own water.

"I would have thought you were a vegan or something," Ty said.

Cassie shook her head. "No. I like meat."

Her words put an image in his head that had no business being there. Thankfully, the server returned and they all ordered their meals.

He managed to keep his mind on his rather excellent burger as the three of them ate. Ty brought up the new addition to the adventure course, which kept Jake talking and his sister listening.

"You have to give it a try, Cassie," Jake said.

She snorted, an adorable sound that made her blush a little. "Not on a bet, bro."

"It's not so scary," Ty put in. "I've run it all."

Her pretty blue eyes ran over his body and her gaze made

his skin sizzle. "You're a daredevil like my brother, I take it?"

Ty grinned. "Maybe a little."

She sipped at her glass of wine. "I shouldn't be surprised, since you're an animal-tamer."

"He's amazing, Cass," Jake said. "I call him the gator whisperer."

Ty felt his cheeks heat. "You just have to know how to handle them. That's all."

Cassie's eyes sparkled at him and he wondered just what she was thinking. Her little pink tongue peeked out again, running over her full lips, and he shifted in his chair. Taking a drag of his beer, he turned his focus to the dormant fireplace at her back.

The three of them hung around a little bit after they finished eating. Ty nursed his beer, more than happy to linger in her company. And Jake's too, of course. He peeled a bit of the label off his beer as he admitted at least to himself that this had everything to do with Cassie and nothing to do with Jake. He wouldn't tell his friend he was stripping the paper off the bottle in response to any sexual frustration he was feeling. Nope.

"Harmony told me you live out in the tent thing?" Cassie folded her arms and leaned toward Ty. "How is that?"

"It's a tent-cabin," Jake said. "It's pretty comfortable, right

Ty? Wired for electricity and running water. Gorgeous setting."

"Nice and quiet, too," Ty said.

Cassie nodded, but she looked skeptical. "Isn't it a little…primitive?"

Ty leaned forward, coming as close to her as he could manage with the round table between them. "You'll have to come out and see it sometime. Judge for yourself."

Her lips parted and he wondered what she was going to say. Would she refuse? Think he was too much of an outdoor guy, given that she was clearly an indoor girl? He read the interest in her eyes, though. Just what was he doing, anyway? Offering her a tour of his place in front of her brother? Real nice.

"Dessert?" Jake said at last.

"None for me," Cassie said. "I wouldn't mind another glass of wine, though."

Ty nodded and signaled for the server.

"I'm gonna take off, then." Jake took out his phone and a grin tugged his lips up at one corner. Ty had no trouble guessing who the text was from. "Claire should be back in a little while." He looked over at his sister. "I hate to drag you away, Cassie."

Her brow furrowed a little and Ty made a snap decision.

"I can take Cassie back to Rick's," he said.

"Thanks, man." Jake stood, and then reached for his wallet.

"It's on me this time," Ty said.

"Thanks again." Jake brushed a kiss on his sister's cheek. "See you soon, sis. And don't worry. You'll do much better tomorrow."

Cassie smiled up at her brother and Ty could see the affection between them. They were a lot alike, her and this brother. She was more reserved, though. A little bit like Rick that way. She was holding herself back. Why, he couldn't guess.

"Work was rough today, huh?" he asked her after Jake left.

She sipped her wine, and then carefully placed the glass back on the table. "I have no clue, Ty. I told you I've never had a job before."

That still floored him. "Just do your best."

A kind of sadness came into her eyes and she sighed. "I'm scared."

"Scared of what?"

"That my best just isn't good enough."

She wore her emotions on her face and he wondered if she knew that.

"Come out to my place tonight." She quirked a brow, so he let a smile play on his lips. "Just for a little while. Check out the view. Listen to the sounds of nature and nothing else."

She brushed her hair back from her face and nodded. "Okay, Ty. You're on."

Chapter 5

Ty drove away from the center of Cypress Corners, bound for his tent-cabin place. Cassie surprised herself with her quick agreement to his suggestion. She was aware of at least one reason she'd wanted to come out to the lakeshore with him tonight, though. She really didn't want to go home to Rick and Harmony's yet. And what better distraction was there than a hot guy with a gorgeous smile?

"The far lakeshore was going to be developed a couple of years ago but they've moved on to other parts of the property," Ty told her, throwing a smile her way. "Good for me, right?"

"Harmony used to live out here," Cassie said. "Then Jake."

"Yep. I like it. I usually stay a couple of nights in the village but most nights I stay out here."

She wondered why that was so. Did he have a girlfriend down here? Did he have commitments beyond his job? She so didn't do commitments of any kind.

She wasn't going to pry into his life, either. She was only in Cypress for a limited time, not that she knew exactly how long that would be. Playing around with Ty would make her time here more than fun. She could guess that from the heat between them from the start. He didn't seem like the type of guy who played, though.

Falling silent, she just sat in his truck as he piloted them down a winding dirt road. It wound through towering trees and she could see the full moon sparkling on the lake as they drew closer to it. The setting looked like something out of a postcard. Wild and beautiful and very serene. She'd never seen anything like it. Not when she'd been bouncing around Europe and not when she'd stayed at nearly every posh resort she could find to lose herself.

She couldn't help but lean closer to the windshield, her eyes taking in every detail that revealed itself. "Oh, it's pretty out here."

Ty made a sound of agreement. "Here it is."

She squinted and could just make out a small cabin-like shape as they drew closer. A light came on, it must have been motion-sensitive, and she could see a sweet little building tucked between the tall trees. It did look like it was half tent half cabin, so now its name made sense to her.

Pulling the truck to a stop, he waited a beat and then faced her. "We're here."

She suddenly felt safe and cozy in his truck. Like she didn't want to leave. His scent was fresh and strong and she wanted to wrap herself in him. There was danger here too, though. This man was very tempting and to more than her sanity.

Thankfully, Ty got out and walked around to her side of the truck. He opened her door and she smiled up at him.

"Ever the gentleman." She grabbed her bag and stepped out. "A girl could get used to this."

He shrugged, stretching the shoulders of his close-fitting Henley. "My mother raised me right."

She laughed. "You're a puzzle, Ty."

He waved her ahead of him with a smile. "Nah, Cassie. I'm easy."

She stepped up onto the small wooden porch, stopping in front of the door. Ty joined her, and then unlocked and opened the door for her.

"Like Jake said, it's not much."

"It's not much but it's home?" she asked with a tilt of her head.

"I don't know. You tell me."

She stepped in as he flicked on a light. Her mouth fell open as she glimpsed the interior. There was a big bed with a black iron head and footboard sporting a crisp taupe comforter. Several pillows were piled on the bed, but there wasn't a ruffle in the place. A rag rug in muted colors covered the wide-plank floor, an unexpectedly cozy touch.

"Harmony lived here? Their house is so pretty and this is…"

"A little too manly?"

"I was going to say plain."

Ty shut the door and turned to her. "Jake managed to undo a little bit of the shabby-chic vibe Harmony had left behind before moving into Claire's for good. I moved in my own stuff when I came here to stay. Kept the rug, though. And the bed."

She wandered around, touching the iron footboard, the deceptively-soft comforter.

"This bed is pretty nice. I would have kept it, too."

She nearly bit her tongue. Why was she playing with this guy? Talking about his bed? He might be fun to flirt with but he just wasn't that kind of guy. She was sure of it.

Beside the bed was a nightstand and a squat dresser with a small mirror on top. There was a tiny desk set against the bare wood framing the interior, and what might be called a kitchen in the other corner. It had a free-standing sink, a small fridge and a wooden table with two chairs.

"You live out here?"

"Most of the time, yes."

She looked around the one room. "Where's the bathroom?"

He chuckled. "Out back. Just a short walk. There's a shower, too."

Her mouth dropped open. "Your bathroom, your shower, is outside?"

"It's all running water, Cassie. Not an outhouse or anything."

She shivered. "Still."

He shrugged. "I wear boots when I go out there. Besides, I know where to step."

She settled down on the side of the bed. "You're not like any guy I've ever known, Ty."

He came closer, and for a second she thought he was going to sit in the chair near the little desk. To her surprise, he sat down right beside her. His thigh was strong against her leg.

"You're different, too," he said.

"Oh?" She blinked up at him. "Have a lot of girls out here, do you?"

He dipped his head but she could see his dimples as he smiled. "Nope."

"So tell me, then. Why do you sometimes live out here and sometimes in the village?"

His mouth thinned, and then he took a breath. "My mother lives with me. She has fibromyalgia and has her good days and bad."

"I'm sorry." She was at a loss regarding his revelation. "That's a lot of responsibility."

"You don't know the half of it," he murmured, staring down at the floor.

She reached out and placed her hand on his. "Animal-tamer? A good son? You're too good to be true."

He lifted his head, his hazel eyes dark. Intense. "I'm no choirboy, Cassie."

Heat washed over her as his gaze dropped to her lips. "Ty."

He brought his face close to hers. "Damn, I want to kiss you."

She lifted her hand to place her palm against his cheek. His skin was warm and his jaw was bristled with stubble. "Kiss me, Ty."

He did, turning slightly to pull her up against him. His body was hard. Hot. Pressing up against his chest, her skin began to tingle. Opening her mouth, she welcomed his tongue when he took control of the kiss.

His big hands moved down to her butt and he turned to pin

her underneath him. Her skirt rode up a little, and one of his hands stroked the back of her thigh.

"Cassie," he rumbled, his mouth against her throat. "You smell so damn good."

She murmured something, she wasn't sure what, and then ran her fingers through his hair as he began to kiss his way down the front of her. Cradling his head, she gasped when he dipped his tongue between her breasts.

"Ty…"

He brought up a hand and cupped one breast, kneading and fondling until her nipples were so tight she ached. Pulling one of the lace cups aside, he palmed her bare breast. Moaning, she arched toward him and was rewarded when he brought that kissable mouth to her breast and suckled.

He was a busy boy and he certainly knew what he was doing. His fingers slipped up and under her panties and she moaned again. Two fingers stretched her, and she felt the tickling of something she'd rarely experienced. She was so close she could hardly breathe.

"Oh, yes," she gasped, squeezing her eyes shut.

Ty continued to lick and nibble on her breast as she began to come. Lights flashed behind her lids and she cried out as she trembled beneath him. A few seconds later, reality hit her. Hard. What had she just done?

Opening her eyes, she found Ty staring down at her. She saw the need on his face, and the sparkle in his gorgeous eyes. Any regret she might have felt for indulging in this guy went flying out one of the tent-cabin's tiny windows.

"Damn," he said again.

She smiled. "Nope. You're certainly not a choirboy."

He growled at her, and then rolled on top of her. His hands bracketed her face and he kissed her. Bringing his brow to hers, he let out a shaky breath. "I had to touch you, Cassie."

She could feel that he was hard in his khakis. And Lord, he felt big.

"I want to touch you, Ty."

***

Ty closed his eyes and whispered a prayer, and then grinned at her as he flipped onto his back.

"Like you said, I'm a gentleman. Who am I to refuse a lady's request?"

Laughing, she trailed her fingers over his chest. Tugging at his shirt, she bared his torso and stroked her hand over his skin. "You're one beautiful man, Ty Walsh."

He chuckled, and then groaned as she lightly scraped her nails over his belly. "Don't play with me, Cassie. I'm real close."

A wicked, delicious glint came into her beautiful blue eyes and her lips tilted up at the corner. "How close?"

"Just touch me, baby." He swallowed thickly. "Please."

She came up on her knees and bent down to kiss his navel. Her hand cupped him through his pants and he moaned again. A couple flicks of her fingers and she had him in her grasp. And at her mercy. She stroked him long and slow.

"Very nice, Ty," she said. "To quote you? *Damn*."

His laughter ended on a long moan. Her fingers were magic on him and he was going to lose it any second. Closing his eyes, he arched toward her. She stroked him, fast and hard, and brought her lips to his. Tasting her, he cupped the back of her head and took her tongue into his mouth. He hadn't lied. He was damn close to losing it but he didn't care.

Her kiss was as sweet as her touch was scorching hot. Again and again she played him, rubbing her beautiful breasts against his chest as she drove him out of his mind. She'd been so hot as he'd stroked her, too. Wet and tight and perfect. He couldn't remember a time when he'd been this wild for a woman. It had to be her. Just her. There was no question about it.

The next second he came hard and fast, bucking as she continued to kiss him crazy. She lifted her head a fraction from his, her lips swollen and her cheeks flushed.

"That was so hot," she murmured.

He brushed his hair back from his face as he slowly caught his breath. Tugging his shirt down over his wet belly, he threw her a look.

"That sure brings back memories," he drawled.

"Oh?" She smiled, cradling her chin in one hand as she settled down on his chest. "Memories of getting all hot and bothered in your truck on a Saturday night?"

"Maybe." He laughed. "But it's been a long damn time, sweetheart."

She lost her smile, an expression of vulnerability on her face for a brief second. Then she brightened. "Then I'll consider myself lucky."

He came up on his elbows. She was mussed and rosy and looked incredible in his bed.

"I'd love to make you a whole lot luckier but I think your brothers would kill me."

Rocking back a little, she stretched out beside him and

leaned up on one elbow. "I'm a big girl, Ty. But maybe you don't want to get tangled up with me."

He turned to face her. "Cassie, believe me. Right now I want nothing more than to get tangled up with you good and hard in my bed."

She tossed her head back, her silky hair brushing over his arm. "You're a little bit of a bad boy, aren't you? Under that good-son nature-boy thing you have going."

He shrugged. "Maybe."

She looked like she wanted to ask him something, but then she gave a small shake of her head. "I should get back. Otherwise Rick and Harmony will have no trouble guessing what I've been up to."

"Would that be a problem?"

She sat up, righting her clothes as she let out another of those sighs of hers. "I've put my family through a lot, Ty. I promised myself I wouldn't be any trouble for them now."

"They love you, Cassie."

She shot him a look of surprise, and then smirked. "They don't know me."

The girl had secrets. That was for sure. He wanted to know her, though. A whole lot more than just naked, too.

"Let me get you home, then." He winked. "I wouldn't want both Chapman brothers beating the shit out of me tomorrow."

That got a little laugh out of her, which he took as the reward it was. "Okay."

The drive back into the village was a quiet one. His body was still sated from their love play but he couldn't help wondering just how great it would be when he finally had her. He would have her, too.

She might not want to bring trouble to her family, but he was pretty good at hiding things himself. He doubted anybody really knew him. Not now. And not in a really long time.

He was dedicated to his work. He was devoted to his mother. He was determined to get Riley into their lives for more than the odd weekend. All of that was true.

But maybe, just maybe, he wanted something for himself for once. And he suspected that Cassie Chapman would be a damn fine thing to have in his life, at least for a little while.

All he had to do was figure out just how to make that happen.

Chapter 6

Ty was still thinking about Cassie the next morning. About how sweet she'd been there in his bed. About how sad she'd looked as she talked about her family. He was tempted to ask her out to the tent-cabin again. To pick up right where they'd left off. Damn, it would be so good.

Forcing his mind back to the present, he parked the truck and made his way into the Sales Center. He had that tour to give to the prospective sales staff and he could use the focus. It would be healthier for him to think about the property and its attributes and not the attributes of a certain brunette, especially since he was going to report back to that brunette's big brother.

"Hey, Ty."

Ty looked up to see Rick Chapman standing in the lobby. Schooling his expression, he smiled at his friend. It wouldn't do for Rick to know Ty was having all sorts of racy thoughts about the guy's little sister.

"Hey."

Rick crossed his arms. "Ready for today's tour?"

"Sure. Listen, how much do you want me to tell these people?"

Rick smiled. "Don't scare them. I'm thinking about bringing

a few of them on and I need them to willingly lead property tours."

Ty laughed. "I'll keep it tame. I promise."

"Cool. They're over by the scale model."

Ty nodded and headed over to the topographic table display depicting the sprawling development. The Center's interior was painted in greens and decorated with photos of Cypress Corners. It was built like an estate home, plush and inviting and very different from the Cypress Institute.

He joined the other people standing around the table as the tour guide's voice droned on from a far corner. He caught bits of the presentation, aimed to draw people to the very contradictions Ty liked about the place. A championship golf course and five-star restaurant bracketed by pristine lakes and a pet park. Close to seven thousand acres dedicated to the conservation of native plants and animals. It spoke to him and, if he could get the salespeople to project that excitement when they give their own property tours? It would mean success for the development and the perpetuation of the Institute's mission as well.

He tuned out the murmurs from the prospective sales staff and looked at the miniature layout of Cypress Corners on the table. Although he'd explored just about every corner he felt at times like he was still learning about the property, even four months after starting here. He could spot the village where the house he shared with his mother sat easily enough, but he couldn't keep his gaze from drifting to the other side of the table at the far lakeshore. His tent-cabin wasn't there but he figured he'd always have a fondness for that little patch of land. The small camp, the narrow dock that jutted out onto the lake. The view in the morning as mist drifted up off the water and the sun rose behind him. He wanted to share that view with Cassie. After spending the entire night loving each other until they collapsed in exhaustion.

"Good morning," Rick said. "Allow me to introduce Tyler Walsh. He's Cypress Corner's Wildlife Technician and Eco-tour Guide."

The six people clustered around the table murmured their greetings, which Ty returned. Big, white smiles struck him. They all looked like they stepped off a billboard or one of those real estate signs at a bus stop.

"Are you all set for an adventure this morning?" he asked them.

The group, four guys and two girls, exchanged nervous looks. They looked to be in the mid- to late-twenties, and just about as polished as Tammy. From the tales Harmony had shared a couple of the times Ty had been over at their house, Rick had been just as starched and polished to a sheen when he'd first come down to Cypress. There was still that air of remoteness from Rick now and then, something he had in common with his little sister. Once again, Cassie popped into his head. He had to get her out of there and fast.

"Let's saddle up, then," he said.

By their shocked expressions, he figured they took him at his word. Chuckling, he shook his head.

"Let's go out to the cart," he clarified.

Once more, he was greeted by big bright salespeople smiles.

"I'll leave you to it, Ty," Rick said. "Just bring them back alive."

Ty laughed again and led the group out to the waiting electric vehicle parked at the curb. It was an eight-seat, oversized golf cart with a striped canopy. It would be just perfect for today's excursion, since he didn't plan on leaving the pavement with this group. God only knew what they would do if he did.

As they buckled themselves in, he mentally reviewed the tour he planned to give today. He would focus on the points that would most appeal to folks looking to move here. The salespeople would be familiar with the neighborhood school and parks, as he knew Rick had arranged tours for them much like the sales staff gave every day. Channeling the Crocodile Hunter, Ty began his spiel as he drove away from the town center toward the east side of the property. Except for the accent, of course.

He would show them a bit of the wild side. He smiled to himself. But just a little bit. To give them a taste of what could be experienced here. And if they bought into the concept? He'd make a note of it and let Rick know just who would do their best to sell it to investors and future residents.

After he'd shown them as much nature as could be experienced from the roadside, he fielded questions.

A few of them asked some insightful ones about energy expenditures and the conservation projects currently underway. One of the guys, probably the oldest in the group, asked about rate of return on investment. Okay, that wasn't his thing and he wouldn't hazard a guess.

After about an hour and a half, he could see them flagging. He guessed they were eager to get back to the safety of the Sales Center and Ty was ready to do some exploring on his own. He'd blocked out a couple of hours after lunch to explore more of the east side, places where you couldn't drive a golf cart.

Pulling up in front of the Sales Center, he shut off the cart and stood once more.

"Mr. Chapman will give you my contact info. If you have any other questions or you'd like to take another tour, don't hesitate to call on me."

One of the women, a serious-looking thing who'd seldom looked up from her tablet during the tour, raised a hand.

"Mr. Walsh, do you offer more adventurous tours?"

The other woman and one of the younger men snickered a little but Ty knew she wasn't referring to anything racy.

"I do. If you come by the Cypress Institute you can sign up for a tour of the wilder parts of the property."

Her eyes sparkled and he made a mental note to keep an eye out for this one. She'd been quiet but seemed to absorb everything he'd said about the importance of conservation and the mission of the Institute as well.

"Thank you, I will," she said.

They got out of the cart and filed into the center. Rick was waiting once more in the lobby.

"Go ahead and grab a water or soda out of the fridge in the break room," he told them. "We'll meet in the conference room in about ten minutes."

Chattering among themselves, they went down the hallway. Rick faced Ty. "What do you think? Any standouts?"

Ty nodded. "The one guy with the buzz cut. He seemed keen on the energy conservation aspects."

Rick nodded. "Good, because we're going to offer more of the smaller homes with optional systems like solar and geothermal. Anyone else?"

"The glasses girl. She's got a spark of something, Rick. I think she can get really excited about the natural aspects if given the chance."

"Enthusiasm is half the battle." Rick nodded. "This was terrific, Ty. I'll get with them and pick their brains to see just what they got from the tour."

"It was painless, really," Ty told him. "Although I was itching to off-road and give them a real tour."

Rick laughed. "Save that for after they've been here a while."

Ty nodded with a smile. "You got it. I'm heading over to the Institute to check in with the director."

"Tell Cassie I said hey," Rick said.

Ty began to protest, and then realized that Rick knew he'd know she was working there. "Sure."

Heading back out, he crossed the street and entered the Institute. Cassie was there at the receptionist desk and clearly in the weeds again. The phone was beeping and the desk was a mess. Stepping close to the desk, he cleared his throat and she looked up. For just a second, if he blinked he would have missed it, she shot him a look of excitement at seeing him. Then her face crumbled and she sank into her chair.

"Rough morning?" he asked.

"I think I'm going to single-handedly bring this operation to a screeching halt."

Ty laughed. "Come get a cup of coffee with me. You can take a break, can't you?"

"If I get somebody to take the phone."

"I'll do it," Harmony said.

Ty smiled at Rick's wife as Cassie shot her a look of extreme gratitude.

"I love you, Harmony," she said. "Have I told you that I love you?"

Harmony laughed lightly. "About five times this morning."

"You saved me. About five times this morning." Cassie stood. "And now I can definitely use a shot of caffeine. What can I get you?"

Harmony wrinkled her nose for a second, and then nodded. "Today I'll do a caramel macchiato. Grande, I think."

Cassie grabbed her mammoth purse from one of the desk drawers. "You got it." She faced Ty. "Let's go."

Ty raised his brows. "Ladies first."

She flashed him a smile and he felt it hit him just right. Whistling, he followed her out the door. He'd just ignore the speculative look on Harmony's face. He was just taking a friend out for a cup of coffee. That was all.

If he wanted to spend more than a coffee break with Cassie, that was his business.

And he was really good at keeping his business his own.

***

Cassie could have hugged Ty when he'd appeared at her desk. Heck, she could have wrapped herself around him given half the chance.

"Thank God Becky comes back tomorrow," she said as they entered the coffee shop.

"Where will you go then?" Ty asked.

"I have no idea. I have to work. Maybe Rick can use me in the Sales Center."

Ty nodded, and then stepped up to the counter. He ordered a

latte and Cassie gave her and Harmony's orders. Stepping to the side to wait for their drinks, he leaned against the counter. She felt a little self-conscious about her appearance this morning. She was a little mussed and rumpled, but that couldn't be helped. He, on the other hand, looked delectable.

"What were you up to this morning?" she asked.

He grinned. "I took some of your brother's prospective hires out for a tour."

"I need to take one, I guess. I suppose if I'm going to work for Rick, I'll have to."

His brows raised. "I didn't give a sales tour, though. I took them out toward the wild side of the property." His dimples appeared. "Not too wild, though. I don't think they could have handled it."

She ran her gaze over him. He wore a polo shirt in a green that made his eyes light up golden and bright. His jeans, as usual, hugged his legs just right. "Do you think I could? Handle it, I mean?"

His eyes lit and she nearly bit her tongue. Oh, she was going to hell for sure, teasing this man in the coffee shop of all places.

"I'd say you could handle anything, Cassie."

His words were innocent enough but his tone was deep and

a little husky. Was he thinking about what they'd done last night, too?

Luckily, the girl behind the counter called their names and Ty handed Cassie her drink, and then grabbed Harmony's and his own.

"Do you have to get right back?" he asked.

"I think I should." She shook her head. "But I suspect it can only be a good thing if I stay out of the place."

He lifted his chin to indicate she should go in front of him and the two of them stepped out into the courtyard.

"Becky will be back tomorrow," he said.

Cassie eyed him. "Do you know Becky very well?"

She'd tried to sound off-hand but wasn't sure she pulled it off.

"Not very. She's been at the Institute for some time, though."

"You've never had her out to the tent-cabin?"

His eyes widened. "Nope."

Just that one word put her fears to rest. What was she thinking, anyway?

"Look, I have no right to ask you about your dating habits, Ty."

He shrugged one of those big shoulders of his. "Like I told you, I'm no choirboy. I'm also not a man whore, either."

She laughed. "Good to know."

"And a damn shame," Lettie said to their right.

The woman was watching them, a small smile on her patrician features. Cassie felt her cheeks flame but she held herself steady.

"Good morning, Lettie," she said.

"Good morning, Cassie dear." Lettie's eyes ran over Ty. "And Tyler Walsh, you're looking mighty fine this morning."

"Good to see you, Mrs. Fairfax."

She laughed, a throaty easy sound. Cassie found herself smiling.

"Oh, Ty! You don't have to be so formal with me. You forget I'm close friends with your mama."

"Know all my secrets, do you?" he teased.

Lettie's eyes sparkled. "Oh, I know lots of secrets. Everyone knows I pride myself on being the soul of discretion, however."

Despite the woman's words, Cassie wasn't going to divulge a thing to her. Not about Ty and not about her own mess she'd left behind when she'd run here.

"Well, I have to get back to the Institute," she said. "Have a good one."

"You too, dear." Again, Lettie eyed Ty. "You too."

Ty chuckled as they made their way back to the Institute. "Lettie's a character. She is a good friend to my mom, though."

"She keeps things interesting," Cassie offered. "That's for sure."

Ty once more let her take the lead as they entered the Institute. At the sight of her desk, her heart sank a little bit. Then she stepped around and saw that everything was neat and tidy. Her sister-in-law wasn't to be found, though.

Taking Harmony's drink from Ty, she placed it and hers on the desk. "Harmony?"

Harmony popped in from just down the hall. "I forwarded the calls to my desk and straightened up. I hope you don't mind."

Cassie could have kissed her. "Not in the least."

Harmony bit her lip, and then smiled. "Why don't you take the rest of the day, Cassie? Becky will be back tomorrow and we have a light day today."

Cassie exchanged a knowing look with Ty, and then slid Harmony a smirk. "And you don't need to fix and straighten again, is that it?"

"Sorry, sweetie." Harmony took her coffee cup and breathed in. "Mmm, thanks for the coffee. Now, go. Go home and take it easy."

Cassie's heart sank all the way to her toes this time. "I always take it easy."

"What?" Harmony asked.

Cassie beamed a smile at her. "Nothing. Thanks, Harmony. For everything. I think I'll take the afternoon to figure out my next job."

"Rick wants you to come by the Sales Center tomorrow."

Cassie nodded. "I know. I should take the tour today."

"That's a great idea," Harmony said.

"I'll walk you over," Ty said.

"And give Lettie more ammo? I don't think so."

Ty frowned a little, and then shrugged. "Anything the lady wants. After all, I'm a gentleman."

His words reminded her of last night in his bed. He'd given control over to her and she'd played with him to her heart's content. She wanted to be in his company for just a little while longer. She could admit that to herself. It was a bummer that she had to admit that in front of Harmony, though.

"Oh, okay. I can't say no to a gentleman."

Ty smiled and they left the Institute.

"You can't say no, huh?" he teased, his voice low.

"Never mind." She sipped at her coffee. "Just so you know, saying no has never been my problem."

He arched a brow and she waved her free hand. "Not like that!" she rushed out. "Jeez, you're going to think I'm as easy to make as a sandwich."

"No, Cassie." He wore that intense expression she'd seen last night. "I don't think that."

She met his gaze and the sidewalk tilted a little bit beneath her. He was so tempting. She hadn't been lying, though. Saying no was never her problem. Saying no to more drinks, no to off-the-hook parties and no to bad boys she just should have ignored had never been the usual for her. Those were things she'd agreed to in a heartbeat, to her regret now. Ty, though? He was in a completely different class.

She wanted to say yes to Ty. Over and over again.

Chapter 7

By the end of the week, Ty felt like he was about to crawl out of his skin. After leaving Cassie in her brother's capable hands at the Sales Center, he'd gone hiking in the wilder parts of Cypress to lose himself. And work off his frustration. Just being near her made his blood heat. After about an hour he couldn't hide any longer but at least she was no longer at the Institute to drive him crazy when he'd gone back there.

He'd smelled her scent, though. That flowery sweet smell of her that had lingered on his sheets after she'd left that first night. When Becky had taken up her post again on Wednesday, he'd been relieved and not just because he would be sure to get his messages.

He'd caught glimpses of Cassie a couple of times, though. Coming or going from the Sales Center. Dressed and polished and looking like a female version of Rick. He liked her mussed and rumpled much better, though. Maybe he should suggest to Rick that she take one of the eco-tours with him. That would mess her up a little bit. She looked so unapproachable when she was pressed and starched.

Now it was Friday afternoon and he'd already checked in with Dr. Robbins before heading home. As he stepped out of the

Institute he heard someone call his name. Glancing over at
Lettie's favorite table, he saw his mother sat there as well. She
was wearing a big smile he couldn't help but return as he made
his way along the walk toward them.

"Hi, Mom. Mrs. Fairfax."

Lettie nodded and his mother clasped her hands in obvious
delight. "We're getting Riley overnight, Ty!"

His mouth dropped open. "That's terrific. Why?"

She frowned at him. "Why? I don't know why. I didn't ask."

Ty turned a free chair around and straddled it, facing the two
women. He knew his mother confided in Lettie and had no
qualms about discussing Riley in front of her.

"There has to be a reason Hank is suddenly being
magnanimous."

"I'm taking it for the gift it is, son. We'll have our little girl
from tomorrow morning until you bring her back on Sunday."

"What time?"

Ty knew Hank never left things open-ended. Not where
Tracy's family was concerned. His mother fiddled with her
napkin.

"Mom?"

"You have to pick her up at ten o'clock tomorrow morning

and bring her back at five o'clock on Sunday afternoon."

He thought for a minute. Hank had to have something lined up for Saturday night. Something loud and rowdy that would call his friends on the police force to come out and quickly dismiss.

"Linda must be going out of town," he guessed out loud.

"I guess so," his mother said. "She takes such good care of Riley, though."

Ty couldn't argue with that. Hank's long-suffering wife was very good with Riley if a little cold. He couldn't really blame her, though. She'd raised his kids to adulthood and then her husband brings home the child of his barely-legal late girlfriend? It had to be a lot to take.

"Then we have to make sure we give Riley a good time," he said.

His mother beamed at him. "Maybe we can have a picnic out by the lake."

Ty shook his head. "That might be too much, Mom. Let's just play it by ear?"

"Did I hear someone mention a picnic?" Harmony called as she approached the table.

Ty smiled at Rick's wife. "We have Riley this weekend."

Harmony smiled. "Oh, your sister's little girl! Then that

settles it. You're coming to the barbeque we're having on Sunday. You will have her on Sunday, won't you?"

"All afternoon," his mother answered. "And we would love to come. What can we bring?"

"Just yourselves and that sweet little girl. I don't think I've seen her but once. Rick will be pleased you've finally relented about coming to our house on a Sunday."

He acknowledged to himself that he'd avoided going to Rick's house for their frequent Sunday get-togethers every time they'd asked him. He had his reasons, though. Most Sundays his mother was tired from trying to make their time with Riley the best ever. And just as often, he'd been so pissed and guilty that he'd had to take the little girl home to Hank yet again.

He'd never had better friends than the Chapmans, but he and his mother had so little time with Riley that he hadn't been able to show her off to his friends like he'd always wanted to. Ty wanted to decline this time, though. Not because he was stingy with the little girl's company. No. Because Cassie would be there and how would she feel with him and his family horning in on them? And, worse, what if Rick and Harmony thought he only accepted this time because Cassie was there now?

"We'll be happy to come, Harmony," he said. "Thanks so

much."

"Terrific. Wait until I tell Rick!"

Harmony hurried over to the Sales Center and Ty knew it would soon be set in stone. He was going to the Chapmans' house on Sunday and taking Riley with him.

"It'll be good for Riley to be around their sweet boy, Nick," Lettie said.

"Oh, yes," his mother said. "I don't think she's around many children near her age."

Ty fell silent. No, she wasn't. Riley was kept in that big house with no one for company but a somber stepmother and a cantankerous redneck father.

"I'd better go home and get things ready," his mother said.

Ty reached out to cover her hand with his. "Don't worry about it, Mom. Just tell me what needs to be done and I'll take care of it."

His mother frowned at him. "Now Thomas Tyler, I don't need you babying me."

Lettie's eyes lit with laughter Ty ignored. "I'm not."

"Sharon, listen to the boy," Lettie said. "You don't want to be tired when that pretty little baby comes to visit, do you?"

Ty could have kissed Lettie right then and there.

"No." His mother sighed. "Okay, Ty. Let's go to the market and pick up a few things for our little angel."

Ty nodded his thanks to Lettie as he and his mother left her at her table.

"So what should we make for dinner tomorrow night? Oh, we haven't had Riley over for dinner in such a long time."

"I'm thinking maybe mac and cheese?"

She eyed him, and then smiled. "Her Uncle Ty's favorite, hmm? Okay, mac and cheese it is."

Ty walked with his mother to the market to load up on goodies for Riley. It was good to focus on tomorrow since Sunday was still looming over his head. The barbeque at Rick and Harmony's should be torture.

How was he going to be so close to Cassie without her family, and his mother, guessing just how much he wanted her?

***

Cassie's breath whooshed from her lungs as the little body slammed down onto her.

"Aunt Cassie! Aunt Cassie!" Nick shouted. "Get up, Aunt Cassie!"

Cassie gently shoved him off of her and opened her eyes. "Hey there, Nick."

The little boy beamed down at her, his face close to hers. She gazed into his hazel eyes, so like Harmony's, and smiled. She was starting to feel more comfortable around the bundle of energy but, jeez, it was early.

"What's going on?" she asked.

"We're having a barbeque, Aunt Cassie. And a friend is coming over to play with me this time."

"Oh, yeah?"

Nick hopped off the bed and she threw back the covers.

"Ty is bringing his little girl. Riley," he said.

Cassie stilled, and then swung her legs off the side of the bed. "Ty has a daughter?"

"Not a daughter, Aunt Cassie. A little girl."

She blinked, trying to process what Nick was telling her. If Ty had a daughter that would explain why he only stayed out at the tent-cabin a few days a week. Oh, man. Was it his own personal love shack?

A glance at her phone on the nightstand showed her it wasn't quite eight o'clock. Sunlight slanted through the blinds against the windows and she stretched her arms toward the ceiling.

"Where's your mom?"

"Mommy's making breakfast. Mommy makes great pancakes."

"I bet she does."

"Aunt Claire is bringing treats later, too. Have you had Aunt Claire's cookies?"

"I haven't." She ran a brush through her hair. "Pretty good, are they?"

"Yes. Mommy says they're perfect and Uncle Jake says they're just like Aunt Claire."

Cassie smiled as she pictured her daredevil brother settled with someone like Claire. A woman who was sweet and smart and sharp who could keep Jake on his toes. Cassie was looking forward to spending the day with the family. Ty was coming? And he was bringing a child along? His child?

"So, do you play with Ty's little girl a lot?" she asked Nick.

Nick shook his head and picked up Cassie's brush. "No. She's not here much."

Cassie took the brush from him and ran it through his glossy black hair. "That's too bad."

Nick shrugged. "Mommy's happy they're bringing her today." He squirmed away from the brush and grabbed her hand. "Come on, come on! Pancakes, Aunt Cassie. Pancakes!"

"You go. Let me brush my teeth and stuff and I'll come in a minute."

Nick nodded and dashed out of the room. Alone again, she began to worry about seeing Ty today. She hadn't spoken with him since he'd brought her home after fooling around out at his little place on the far lakeshore. She'd seen him a couple of times that week, but only in passing. Maybe that was a good thing. Rick was trying his damnedest to get her on board in the Sales Center but even he couldn't cram all that information into her head in only a couple of days. She'd never imagined there was so much to learn about the property.

The guest room had its own bathroom and she wondered about Ty and how he managed with his outhouse. Okay, it supposedly wasn't an outhouse. Still, she couldn't imagine going outside to pee and shower. No thanks.

Her bedroom at Rick and Harmony's was very cozy, and decorated with the shabby chic vibe Ty had talked about on Monday night. Smoothing the pretty quilt as she made the bed, she wondered if the stuff here had been out at the tent-cabin. This bed wasn't. She was sure of that. This bed was nice but that one out by the lake? That one was big and comfy and had Ty all over it.

She padded down to the kitchen to find Rick and Nick each digging into a stack of pancakes. Harmony waved the spatula at her as she deposited a few more on the platter in the center of the table.

"Good morning," she said.

"Good morning." Cassie sniffed. "Nick wasn't exaggerating. The pancakes smell delicious."

"Dig in, sis." Rick pulled out a chair for her. "Before Nick and I eat them all."

Cassie laughed as she eyed the towering platter. "That would take some doing."

"You haven't seen these guys eat pancakes," Harmony said.

Cassie walked over to the coffee maker and dropped in a pod. "I grew up with Rick and Jake, remember. Our mom was always making tons of food and I always had to fight to get my share."

Harmony shook her head. "I'm kind of hoping that Claire has a little girl."

"Claire's pregnant?" Cassie asked.

"No, no." Harmony grabbed a coffee cup and handed it to her. "I just meant that when they have a baby it would be nice to balance the scales a little."

Cassie poured and fixed her coffee then sat down at the table. "A little girl would be nice." She took a pancake and began to cut it with the side of her fork. "Speaking of little girls, Nick said Ty has one?"

Harmony blinked at her, and then smiled. "Riley is his sister's daughter. She's about three and a half now, I think. A little doll."

"Is his sister coming today, too?" Cassie asked.

Harmony's gaze slid toward Nick before she gave a little shake of her head. "No."

Cassie sensed there was something more to the story. Was Ty estranged from his sister? She couldn't imagine a guy who took care of his mother wouldn't be close to his sister, too.

"Do you know her?" she asked.

Rick eyed their son, and then put down his fork. "Nick, could you grab the other syrup out of the fridge?" Nick nodded and hopped off his chair to run into the kitchen. Rick leaned forward. "Ty's sister died about two years ago. Riley lives with her father's family in St. Cloud."

"Ty and his mother don't get to see her more than once a week," Harmony said.

"That doesn't seem fair."

106

"That's the way it is," Rick said. "Ty's working on fixing it, though."

Nick came back to the table so the adults dropped the subject. Cassie finished her breakfast and sipped her coffee as she puzzled over this new revelation about Ty. The guy had so much on his plate. His life was complicated and she was in the process of un-complicating her own. That realization was disheartening.

Harmony mentioned that everyone would be here by one, so that gave her time to figure out just how she was going to act around Ty and his family. It was bad enough that she had to hide the fact that she was so attracted to him she wanted to wrap herself around him every time he was near. Now she knew he had more to handle than alligators, and she didn't know how she felt about that. He had a steadiness to him. Beneath that sparkling charm he had going. It was heady and addictive and now that she knew a little more about his life? He was so far out of her league.

Taking her cue from Harmony, she dressed in one of her looser t-shirts and a pair of jeans. She left off the heels and opted for a pair of stacked flip flops. She left her hair down, and it waved nicely. She was so tired of tying it back all week.

She heard Ty when he arrived. She couldn't help it. His deep voice rumbled a greeting from the open French doors and her body tingled. The shuffle of little feet met her ears and a pretty little girl soon stood in front of her. She had blond hair and big blue eyes, which she must have gotten from her father. She had dimples, though. Just like her uncle.

"Hi, there," Cassie said.

"Hi." The little girl peered up at her, her lower lip poked out a little. "I'm Riley."

"It's nice to meet you, Riley."

"Riley, where'd you run off to?" An older woman who could only be Ty's mother stepped out onto the patio. "There you are, angel."

Ty's mother placed a hand on Riley's head, love in her eyes that looked so much like Ty's. Then she met Cassie's gaze. "I'm Sharon Walsh. Ty's mother."

"Hello, Mrs. Walsh." Cassie held out her hand, which Ty's mother shook. "I'm glad you could come today."

"We were so happy to be invited."

Harmony called her over and she smiled at Cassie and made her way to where Rick and Harmony sat at the table. Cassie knew when Ty approached. She could smell him.

"Hey, Cassie."

She ran her gaze up his worn jeans and another Henley stretching across his wide chest to his smiling face. God, those dimples.

"Hey, Ty."

Ty put his hands in the front pockets of his jeans. "How are things going at the Sales Center?"

She snorted. "I don't think a career in sales is in my future. I've always been more of a buyer."

Ty grinned and she swallowed.

"I'm sure your brother will give you some time to get used to it."

"I guess." His eyes flicked over to the backyard, where Nick was showing Riley his fleet of trucks parked on the grass. "Your niece is adorable."

"Thanks."

She waited for him to say more but he just brought his gaze back to hers.

"You don't get to see her much?"

"Cassie, I don't want to talk about it."

Brr. She'd never heard that tone in his voice but she didn't take it personally. She knew it came from a place of pain. And let's face it, she had no clue how to deal with real emotions.

"Okay."

She turned away from him and joined her family on the patio. As her brothers greeted Ty, he seemed to recover what she was coming to think of as his usual charm and friendliness. He hardly took his eyes off of his niece, though. And when the little girl crawled up on his lap to eat from his plate, there was no way Cassie could ignore the love in his expression.

Her stomach sank. She'd seen that love a few times since she'd come down to Cypress Corners. A lot of times, actually. In Rick's eyes when he was with Nick and Harmony. In Jake's eyes when he looked at Claire. It was pure and warm.

Nodding at something Claire said, Cassie sipped at her lemonade. It was tart and sweet, and just like the feeling settling in her stomach.

She'd never had that kind of love. That was for sure. And right now, she doubted she ever would.

Chapter 8

Ty took his mother's Camry Sunday afternoon, with Riley buckled into her car seat in the back. He couldn't seem to shake himself out of the funk he'd found himself in despite being surrounded by friends and family that afternoon. He was still kicking himself even now for the way he'd dismissed Cassie's innocent question. He knew it was due to the frustration he felt every time he anticipated bringing Riley back to her father's.

Cassie had looked both sweet and hot today, too. He loved her hair when it was loose. It made her look so much more open and he wondered just how much he could get her to open up to him. She had her secrets but, after the way he'd all but snapped at her today, he doubted she'd share them with him any time soon.

"Did you have fun at Rick and Harmony's, honey?"

"Yeah. Nick's fun."

Ty smiled and glanced in the rearview mirror. "Nick had fun with you too, I think."

"Can we go there again, Uncle Ty?"

"Sure."

Riley was humming some tune he didn't recognize and he was so grateful that she could be such a happy child. That meant she didn't pick up on his and his mother's worry all weekend. He would do anything to shield the little girl from any pain, and that meant the emotional kind too.

The drive from Cypress Corners to St. Cloud took about ten minutes. Hank lived in a big Victorian in the heart of the city. It was set near the lakefront and, to hear Hank tell it, it had been in his family since the area was settled. Ty didn't know about that but he knew the guy's family had deep roots in the city. Any hint of trouble with the law always seemed to be swiftly swept under the rug for him, since most of the officials were drinking buddies of Hank's. So Hank's record was pristine, even if Ty chose to delve into it. He partied hard and always had. There had probably been another blowout at his place since Riley had been out of his hair all weekend.

Tamping down his anger, Ty pulled down one of the state-named streets toward the lake. Even though he'd grown up here, it always seemed odd that the cross streets in the city were named for states of the union. Almost without exception.

"Is Daddy home?" Riley piped up from the backseat.

"I think so," Ty answered.

"Mommy Linda was sad yesterday."

"She was?"

"Yeah. She was sad because she was leaving."

"Linda left?"

"To visit her sister. Um, I think."

Ty puzzled over that. Linda was about the same age as Hank, approaching fifty. Could her sister have health issues? He doubted Riley would know anything about that, so he let the subject drop. He just hoped Linda was home to greet Riley. The little girl was growing attached to her even if Linda didn't seem to encourage it much. She was caring to an extent but always seemed to keep Riley at arms' length.

Ty pulled the car into the big driveway in front of the house. It did have a prime spot on a rise, directly across the street from the lake. It was a Sunday, so the lakeshore park was bustling with families enjoying the April afternoon. Both the playground and the beach were crowded and apparently people were making use of the charcoal grills to make their Sunday dinner.

Pulling to a stop, he took out the key and sat for a minute. This brooding wasn't like him. And quite frankly, it was starting to piss him off.

"Okay, munchkin. Let's get you home."

He unbuckled Riley and set her down on her feet, and then grabbed her pink Minnie Mouse backpack. Riley took it and scampered toward the house, coming to a stop when Hank stepped out onto the wide front porch.

"Hey there, Walsh," the man said.

Ty looked over at his sister's ex. Hank was built like most of the good old boys in town. Broad and tall but starting to show a paunch in the middle. He had a head full of salt and pepper hair and a trim beard. He ran the feed store on the main street in the city, another thing that had been passed down through generations. His was the busiest in town, and Ty suspected that more than grain and feed was distributed out of the back of the place.

"Hey, Hank."

There was no love lost between them and Ty managed to just be civil in front of Riley.

"Hey there, baby girl," Hank said to Riley.

Riley ran up to him and hugged Hank's leg with one arm. Ty looked for affection in Hank's expression but the guy was very hard to read.

"Go on in and see Mommy Linda." He touched her hair, and then stepped back. "She missed you."

Riley turned to Ty. "Bye, Uncle Ty!"

And in the next moment she disappeared into the big house,

the wooden screen door banging shut behind her.

"What's the schedule this week, Hank?" Ty asked.

Hank pursed his lips, dragging a hand over his buzz cut. "Don't know as yet, Walsh. Give me until midweek. I'll let you know when you can have the girl."

Ty's lips thinned but he didn't argue. There was no point. Florida had no such thing as child custody but instead had time-sharing. And Hank shared no more than the time he wanted to with Tracy's family. As Riley's closest relative, he held all the cards.

"Okay."

His gut roiling, Ty got back in his mother's car and drove back to Cypress. He'd been investigating how to get Riley a more permanent place in their family almost since Tracy died. There was no such term as "custody" in the Florida Statutes nor was there a primary or secondary residential parent designation in the Florida Statutes. With Tracy gone there was no one Hank had to develop a "parenting plan" with to organize Riley's time and visitation. They were pretty much at his mercy and Ty would try his damnedest to make sure they stayed on the guy's good side, even if the guy was about as friendly as a hungry gator.

As Ty approached Cypress he pulled his thoughts away from Riley and the mess Tracy left behind and focused on making up to Cassie for the way he'd spoken to her. Hell, he'd all but ignored her all afternoon.

He'd been surprised to see how easily she interacted with Nick now, given the stiffness he'd seen when he'd dropped her off last week. Kids were like that, though. They wore down your defenses and wormed their little ways into your heart. Riley certainly had. With the first grasp of his finger in her tiny hand.

By the time he walked into the house he shared with his mother, he'd made up his mind to go right back out. Where, he wasn't quite sure. Maybe he'd spend the night out at the tent-cabin.

"Mom?" He hung the keys to her car on one of the hooks by the door to the garage. "Where are you?"

"In here, Ty."

He found her on the couch in the great room, thumbing through one of her decorating magazines. To his eyes she looked tired but not exhausted. The day had done her good, to be out in the fresh air among friends. And Riley. Ty knew how great she felt after time with Riley, even if caring for the little girl could sometimes be too much for her physically.

"Riley is back at Hank's. Safe and sound."

"You're so good with her."

"It's easy." Ty stretched out on the couch beside her. "You had a good time at Rick and Harmony's."

She smiled at him. "They're such nice people, your friends. And that Cassie is certainly a beauty."

"Yes. She is."

"Lettie said you've been squiring her around town?"

Ty arched his brows. "Squiring? Hardly. I picked her up at the airport."

"And drove her home after dinner last week?"

"Mom, are you keeping tabs on me?"

She chuckled and waved a hand. "Not keeping tabs, no. I'm just stating the obvious."

"The obvious? And just what is that?"

"You like her. And she likes you, Ty. I saw the way she looked at you. Like she was thirsty and you were a glass of sweet tea."

He winced. "Mom!"

His mother shrugged. "I can't blame the girl. You're quite delicious, according to Lettie."

"Jeez." Ty blew out a breath. "Listen. Cassie is Rick and

Jake's little sister. I was just helping out my friends."

His mother slanted him a look. "If you say so."

Ty grumbled and came to his feet. "I'm going out, Mom. Do you need anything?"

"Nope. I'm fine." She took a breath and slowly let it out, a smile on her face. "As much as I miss Riley, I'm enjoying the peace and quiet now that our little spitfire is back at her father's."

"I'm thinking about staying out at the tent-cabin tonight."

"Go."

His mother continued to read her magazine.

"You have my cell number?" he asked.

She slid him a look. "Yes, son. I'll call if I need you."

Ty took her at her word and headed back out to the garage. He had no idea where he was going when he got into his truck. That was, not until he drove past Rick's house and saw the slight figure sitting alone on the porch swing.

He pulled up to the curb and stepped out, coming around slowly as Cassie watched him. She was barefoot, one leg tucked under her as she slowly pushed the swing back and forth in the coming twilight.

"Ty." Her voice was as soft as the light around her. "I didn't expect to see you back here."

Ty shrugged. "I feel like I need to apologize for earlier."

She tilted her head, that beautiful hair of hers brushing over one shoulder. "For what?"

He leaned against the railing and faced her. They were alone, and little ears were far way right now. "For being a dick."

She laughed softly. "When, exactly, were you a dick?"

"This afternoon. You asked about how often we get to see Riley. I snapped at you."

She pursed her lips and nodded. "Yes, you did. You also ignored me all afternoon."

He tilted a smile at her. "Believe me, I didn't ignore you. I watched you. I couldn't keep from watching you."

"That's a little creepy," she teased. "I watched you, too. With Riley. You're wonderful with her."

"I love her. We just don't get to have her often enough."

Cassie's brows knit a little bit. He could tell she wanted to ask him for details but was holding herself back. He could guess the reason. She was afraid he was going to snap at her again.

"Come for a ride with me?" he asked.

***

Cassie stared up at Ty, easily reading the sincerity on his

face. He didn't play games, like so many of the guys she'd known all her life. That was a little scary at the moment. She wasn't used to straight-shooting and had no idea how to fire back.

She ran her eyes from his running shoes up over his worn jeans and dark green t-shirt to the top of his sun-streaked head. He looked really good there, leaning against the porch railing. Here to see her and apologize, though there wasn't any need. There was a tenseness between his eyes, though. And she could guess it didn't have anything to do with his supposed rudeness earlier today.

"A ride to where, Ty?"

He shrugged. "The far lakeshore?"

She laughed softly as she came to her feet. "You want to make out in your truck, don't you?"

The grin he gave her brought out his dimples. "Now, why would you think that?"

She came closer, close enough to smell his fresh scent. She thought about the last time they were alone and her body heated. She'd never felt like this around a guy before. It was a little unsettling.

She slid on her new Keds. They were pretty comfortable for

such plain little things.

"Let me just tell Rick I'll be out."

Ty groaned. "Your brother is going to kill me. I'm sure of it."

Now she laughed out loud. She went inside to find her brother and Harmony curled up on the couch. "Hey, I'm going out with Ty for a little while."

Harmony's brow furrowed for a second, and then she smiled. "You don't have a curfew, Cassie. Right, Rick?"

Rick scowled. "Yeah, right."

Cassie flashed her brother a smile and went back out onto the porch. Ty was still standing there, tall and lean and patient. She didn't know what to expect, since he looked like he really needed to talk. But she would bet her Jimmy Choo bag that they'd end up in his tent-cabin before too long.

"So let's go," she said.

He nodded and waved her ahead of him. He was quiet as he drove her through the village, but he wasn't a chatty guy. His hands gripped the wheel and Cassie knew whatever was bothering him was important. She suspected it was about his niece but she couldn't be sure. No real friends meant no real heart-to-hearts about anything that mattered. She had no experience with sharing.

"Thanks for coming with me," he said, finally breaking the silence. "I not good company and my mom is a little tired."

She smiled at his turn of phrase. "Not good company, huh? What did I do to get so lucky?"

He laughed, his shoulders easing a little bit. "You're good for me, you know that?"

That struck her speechless. She'd never been good for anyone. Not really. A good time maybe, but she knew that wasn't what Ty was talking about. She fell silent like he was as the truck made its inevitable way to the far lakeshore.

Pulling the truck to a stop in front of the tent-cabin, Ty shut off the ignition. Tension still radiated from him. She was at a loss when it came to conversation but she could just guess what might ease a little bit of his rigidity.

"Ty," she said, reaching over to touch his hand.

He stared at her fingers, gently stroking over his. "Cassie, I…" He swallowed audibly. "I shouldn't have brought you out here."

She tilted her head. "Then why, exactly, did you?"

He turned to face her fully. His brows were drawn together over his eyes and his lips parted. "I needed to talk, I guess."

She smiled. "Talk, huh? Is that what the kids are calling it these days?"

He visibly eased a little bit more. "Okay, I thought we could get a little tangled, too."

She couldn't help but remember his admission the last time they'd been alone together. Leaning closer to him, she reached out to push her fingers through his hair until she held his head in her hands. "Let's get tangled, Ty." Bringing her face to his, she brushed his mouth gently with hers. "We can talk…after."

Chapter 9

Ty growled softly and grabbed her to him. His arms wrapped around her and he was strong against her. His body was still rigid, though. She could guess what was bothering him but he was the strong, silent type. She'd seen that before. Even when he was flashing those adorable dimples she could feel it. But now? With him so close against her? She wanted to make him lose a little bit of that control she knew he held onto so tightly.

"Come inside with me," he said, his lips on her throat. "Please."

She squeezed her eyes shut and let her head fall back. "Yes."

He somehow opened his door and pulled her out with him, and then hip-checked the door shut. She just clung to his broad shoulders, wrapping her legs around his waist to lock her ankles. Cupping her butt in his hands, he held her close as he took long strides across the sandy path and up the steps to the tent-cabin. He set her down and she stood on shaking legs.

"We'll take it slow, Cassie."

"That's smart." She stared into his hazel eyes, and the planks beneath her seemed to sway a little. "A nice, slow tangle."

His eyes flared. He let out a low whistle and unlocked the door. They entered the tent-cabin and Ty lit a couple of lamps. She made her way to his very nice, iron bed and kicked off her sneakers. Settling down, she pulled off her t-shirt.

"Damn," he said, staring hard enough to burn holes through the lace cups of her periwinkle blue bra.

Coming up on her knees, she made a circular motion with one finger at him. "Take that shirt off, cowboy."

He chuckled a little and glanced down at the floor. "I'm not a cowboy, Cassie."

"Do you know how to ride a horse?"

He faced her dead on now, his eyes sparkling. "I do." He pulled his shirt up and over his head. "That doesn't make me a cowboy."

She shrugged, her eyes running over every dip and ripple in his amazing torso. His jeans dipped down just enough to show a sliver of light skin right above the waistband.

"Let me have my fantasy, will you?" she teased.

He toed off his sneakers and slowly walked toward her. His narrow hips rolled in his low-slung jeans. "Do you need a fantasy, Cassie?"

She used to, yeah. She used to need flash and show to even

begin to want a guy. Not now, though. Not with Ty.

She gave a slow shake of her head. "With you right here in front of me? You're fantasy enough, believe me."

He might think she was just doing a little bit of dirty talking but she was dead serious. He was more beautiful than any guy she'd ever seen, in person or in the movies. All golden and sculpted and hers for the next hour or so.

He came closer, covering her until she edged back on the bed. He was so big yet he supported himself on his strong arms and stared down into her eyes.

"If I'm a fantasy you're a wet dream," he rasped.

It wasn't poetry but his words sent a tingle over her skin. She was prickly and achy and it was all due to this particular guy. "Oh, my."

He flashed her a quick smile, and then set his mouth on hers. He tasted so good. Fresh and little minty. She took his tongue in her mouth, arching up as she wrapped her arms around his neck. His hair was so soft against her fingers as she ran he hands over his head. When he dipped his head to nuzzle her throat, she let out a purr.

Coming up on his knees, he began to unfasten her jeans. "I have to get you out of these."

She leaned up on her elbows. "What about yours?"

He shot her look of pure heat. "I have to keep mine on for now, sweetheart."

"Okay." She smiled, her breath coming fast. "For now."

He growled again and she shimmied her hips to help him pull off her jeans. Her panties, just a scrap of lace in the same color as her bra, followed. His lips did, too. Following his fingers as he pushed her panties down over her legs. He didn't waste another second before bringing those talented lips of his right to her center.

"Ty!"

He didn't answer with more than a moan as his tongue and lips drove her swiftly to the edge. If she thought he'd been skilled with his fingers the last time they were together he was freaking gifted with that mouth of his.

Higher and higher she climbed, almost frightened by the intensity of the orgasm screaming its way toward her. She must have sobbed or made some kind of sound because he lifted his head as his fingers kept up his sweet torture.

"That's it, Cassie." He licked her clit and she bucked as a kick of sensation struck her. "Come for me."

She reached up over her head to grab onto the iron rails of

the headboard and just let go, crying out as she began to come. He didn't let up. His mouth and the light rasp of the stubble on his jaw sent her out of her mind.

Tremors still rocked her body minutes later as he came up to kiss her lips. "Damn, sweetheart. You're amazing."

"That was…" She was breathing hard now. "That was like nothing I've ever felt before."

He tilted his head, a smile curving his lips. "You came last time."

Her cheeks heated a little bit, which was ridiculous. She was just about naked and he'd just sent her to heaven with his mouth and fingers.

"I never really had orgasms before, Ty." She cupped his cheek with one hand. "Before you, that is."

He pulled back to stand at the side of the bed. "Seriously?"

She came up on her knees again. "I know I might look easy, but I'm not the party girl everyone seems to think."

He placed a knee on the bed. "Sweetheart, you don't look easy. Believe me. As for everyone in Cypress? No one is saying a word about you."

Relief nearly took her breath. "I was worried that my family might hear something they shouldn't."

"About me?"

She shook her head. "Oh no, Ty. Not about you. Everybody loves you. I'm just scared that what happened before will follow me down here."

"What happened before?"

She toyed with the seam of the comforter, her eyes downcast. "You know about the papers, Ty. The pictures."

"I heard something, yes. But from what I know about your family, they trust you. They care about you. You might say they don't know you but I can tell they love you."

She covered her face with her hands. "This is suddenly getting way too personal."

He grasped her wrists and gently pulled her hands away. "Too personal? I just tasted you, Cassie. I just made you come so hard your screams probably scared the owls out of the trees."

She laughed in spite of herself. "Yeah, you did."

He kissed her then. Tenderly. "Anything you tell me stays between us." He ran his eyes over her body and whistled again. "And anything we do together stays between us. You have my word."

"Oh?" She came up to cuddle closer to him. "Were you a boy scout, then?"

He covered his heart with his hand. "Guilty."

As she moved closer she could feel against her belly just how hard he was in his jeans. She placed teasing kisses on his chest. His ridged abs. "Then let's get very personal."

He stood as she placed her hands on the top button of his fly but he stayed very close. "How personal?" His voice was rough. Needy.

She undid first one, and then two of the buttons. He was cut, with those smoking hot indentations just above his hips.

"I want to taste you, Ty."

He trembled at her touch.

"Lord save me," he murmured.

***

On Tuesday morning Ty stood in his kitchen, pouring himself a cup of coffee. He placed the pot back on the burner and brought the cup to his lips. He'd bought his mother a one-cup coffee maker last year but she resisted using it. He admitted that the scent of brewing coffee made the hassle of cleaning the pot and basket almost worth it.

His hair was still damp from his shower and he was dressed for work. He'd slept here last night. In his big bed in the big bedroom on the second floor. Not like Sunday night, when he'd crashed out by the lakeshore after driving Cassie home. One reason was that he didn't want to wake his mother when he came in. Her bedroom was on the first floor and he knew she had trouble sleeping some nights. Another reason was that he just couldn't resist heading back out to the tent-cabin and reliving everything he and Cassie had shared.

Damn, she'd surprised him. Not with her passion, no. She was made for loving, and her body reacted to his every touch. No, she'd stunned him with her confession of the lackluster sex she'd had in her life.

Not that he didn't feel damn good for making her scream like the wind during a summer storm. Still, she must have tangled with some morons. Or maybe they were just selfish. That was probably the case, since he'd gathered from the few times Jake or Rick had talked about her before her arrival she palled around with fancy boys who were as into themselves as much as anyone else.

"I'm surprised to see you here this morning," his mother said.

Ty looked up as she walked toward the kitchen and sat at the tall counter. She folded her hands in front of her, looking at him expectantly.

"Coffee, Mom?" he asked.

She nodded. "Yes, please. And don't change the subject."

He poured her coffee and fixed it the way she liked it, cream and a packet of sweetener, and placed it on the granite counter. "You and I watched TV together last night. Why would you think I would head out to the lakeshore after?"

She took a sip and, if he wasn't mistaken, a small smile played over her lips. "I thought you might want to spend more time out there in your love shack."

"Mom!" Thank God he hadn't been drinking his coffee just then. He would have spewed it all over the counter. "Jeez. Where did you get the idea that it's my…love shack?"

Her gaze grew serious. "Thomas Tyler Walsh. Do you think I don't know you're a red blooded man?"

Ty blew out a breath. "You've been hanging around Lettie too much."

She took another sip of coffee, and then waved a hand. "I know you go out there with girls. It's no big deal."

"Girls? No."

"Women, then. I bet you've taken a few women out there since we've lived in Cypress Corners."

He hadn't but he still felt his face heat. "I'm not going to talk about this with you."

"Ty, you're a man. You have needs."

Ty was seized with the urge to cover his ears and sing to himself very loudly. Maybe a verse or two of Row, Row, Row Your Boat. "Can we drop this?"

"I just want to know you're being a gentleman."

He blinked as he tried to follow his mother's reasoning. "What?"

"You know. Taking care of the girl. I mean, woman."

Now he covered his face with his hands, stifling a groan. "Mom, please."

"You need to take care of her needs too, Ty. She's new to Cypress and might be easily hurt."

He peeped an eye through his fingers. "Who are you talking about?" As if he didn't know.

"Cassie Chapman. I saw the sparks between you two." She grinned. "Wait until I tell Lettie."

"Don't you dare. Cassie doesn't want anyone gossiping about her."

"Ah ha!"

He bit back a curse. She'd caught him.

"I knew you were seeing her. 'Just picked her up at the

airport, Mom.' Right. 'She needed a ride home, Mom.' Hmm?"

"All right, I'm seeing her. I guess. We haven't gone on a real date or anything yet, though."

"So you're just bringing her out to your love shack? That's not the way to charm a woman."

"Please stop calling it my love shack?"

"I didn't realize I'd raised such a prude. You know, when your father was alive we really burned up the sheets."

"Kill me now." He rolled his eyes heavenward. "Please kill me now."

"Oh, all right." She was still smiling, though. "I won't talk to you about this."

"Thank you. And please don't say anything to Lettie?"

"About your love shack?"

He grunted a little. "About Cassie, Mom."

"I'm just teasing. Of course I won't say a thing about that dear girl. You know, there's a story there. A sad one, I'm sure. Why else would she stay away from her family all that time?"

"I'm not really sure."

Actually, Ty had heard about the tabloids and racy pictures but had no idea what had happened to ultimately bring her here and no idea what had kept her away so long before. Maybe if he'd had a brain cell still firing after Cassie had blown his mind they would have had that talk he'd anticipated. In the end, he hadn't shared any of his frustrations and she hadn't spilled any of her own secrets. Other than her previous lack of orgasms, that was.

He drained his cup and put it in the sink. "I've got to go. I have three tours today."

"Okay, dear. Take care."

He kissed her cheek and walked toward the door to the garage. "Bye."

"You know I love it when you stay here at the house, Ty. But I don't mind it at all when you take time for yourself."

He met her gaze and saw the unconditional love she had for him. "Thanks. I think."

He heard her humming as she drank her coffee, probably plotting how to drive her son crazy with some future inappropriate conversations.

By the time he parked the truck he'd finally managed to put their odd and uncomfortable exchange out of his head. Love shack? He'd never actually taken a woman out there before Cassie. He'd just thought of it as a place to crash if he stayed out late or had a really early morning the next day. He was no choirboy, true. He hadn't lied to Cassie about that.

He'd grown up in St. Cloud and there were a few notches on his belt. Whenever he'd needed to get out he'd just hit one of the few bars that dotted the city. Maybe he'd have a couple of beers. Shoot a few games of pool. And maybe he'd hook up with a woman who happened to be looking for the same thing he was. A couple of hours of sex without any lingering attachment. But he didn't go out looking to get laid. Not in a while, anyway. And any time he'd gotten laid it had been in town. Far from Cypress and far from his mother.

He walked into the lobby of the Cypress Institute and smiled at the redhead behind the reception counter. He couldn't help but picture Cassie in that seat. Up to her eyebrows in papers and phone calls. She'd been mussed and adorable and that just might be the first time he felt the sizzle of attraction. No. That was when he'd pulled his truck up to the curb at the airport.

"Mr. Walsh." The woman greeted him with a smile. "Good afternoon."

"We've talked about this, Becky. Call me Ty? Mr. Walsh was my father."

"Thomas Tyler Walsh." She smiled. "And you're the third."

Ty chuckled. Everyone seemed so impressed that he was the

third. He wore his father's name, and his grandfather's name, proudly but those good men were gone. To him it was just a name. Now.

"Yeah, yeah. Is the director in?"

Becky nodded.

"Great. Thanks." He headed down the hall to Dr. Robbins' office.

"Good morning, Ty." The director met him in the hallway. "You have a full schedule today, I see."

"Three tours, yes. All on the east side."

Dr. Robbins nodded, his brows beetled. "Have you taken Rick's sister out there yet?"

Ty's mouth dropped open. The director couldn't be talking about the far lakeshore. Could he?

"On a tour?"

"Yes, on a tour." Dr. Robbins blinked at him. "I know she's at the Sales Center now and, as much as I appreciated the effort she put in here at the Institute, I think that might be a better fit for her."

"Maybe." Ty smiled. "Today's tours will be a little wild for a city girl, though. Tomorrow I have a tame nature tour planned for the afternoon. I can put on that one."

"Good, good."

With that, the director turned and headed back into his office. Ty knew the man's mind was always working, so he didn't take any offense at the dismissal.

He thought about having Cassie on tour with him tomorrow. Sitting there on the cushioned seats, holding on tight as they bounced over the rougher terrain. Clutching the sides of the eco-tour gator vehicle like she'd held onto the iron railing of his bed. Her body moving in rhythm to the cart's every move. Just like she'd responded to his.

He blew out a breath. Maybe he'd take the smoothest paths tomorrow. He didn't want to sport a hard-on in front of the rest of the group. That would be a bit too back-to-nature for Cypress Corners.

Shaking his head, he crossed over to the lot beside the Sales Center again and tried to focus on the upcoming tour. It wasn't going to be easy. First the out-of-body experience of talking about sex with his mother and now picturing Cassie in the flesh?

It was going to be a long day.

Chapter 10

It was going to be a long day.

Cassie pulled her hair back into the sleek ponytail she'd worn to work this morning and tucked her rumpled blouse back into her dress pants. She'd had one hell of an afternoon.

"You'll get the hang of it, Cassie," Tammy, saleswoman extraordinaire, said from her perch at one of the tables in the break room.

Cassie let out a breath and grabbed a bottle of water out of the fridge, and then faced Tammy. The cool, calm and collected woman sat sipping an iced tea. What was that southern saying? Butter wouldn't melt in her mouth, maybe? She'd have to ask Lettie. She was always handing out nuggets of wisdom to anyone who asked. And many who didn't.

"Easy for you to say. You didn't just almost kill four people."

Tammy laughed, flipping her perfect hair over on shoulder. Cassie used to be able to pull off that move. Before the heat and humidity of Florida gave her hair waves she hadn't known she had.

"Rick has faith in you."

"Then he's delusional." She cracked open the bottle and

took a long drink. "It wasn't really my fault, though. That thing ran across the path and scared the hell out of me."

"What thing?"

"I don't know what it was. A weasel, maybe. An otter? It was long and slinky and covered with fur."

Tammy shrugged. "I have no idea what it could be. You should ask Ty."

Cassie nodded. "Yeah, he should know. I swear the guy knows everything."

Tammy eyed her closely then, her perfect brows drawn together. "Have you been spending a lot of time with Ty?"

Cassie took another drink to cover up whatever stammering answer she might have made otherwise. She mimicked Tammy's nonchalant shrug and capped her water.

"He sure knows his stuff," she said. That sounded naughty. "I mean, he is the nature guy around here."

Tammy smiled. "Yeah, that's what I thought."

Cassie was about to ask the woman what she meant when Claire walked in.

"Hey there, ladies." Her eyes went wide when she took in Cassie's flushed cheeks and mussed appearance. "What happened to you?"

Cassie rolled her eyes. "I've been at the Sales Center for almost a week and I still have no clue how to competently lead a property tour."

"An animal ran her cart off the path," Tammy provided.

"What kind of animal?" Claire asked.

"Apparently Ty will know," Tammy went on. "Cassie's going to ask him."

Tammy was teasing a little bit but was she also interested in Ty? What woman wouldn't be, but still. He had said he wasn't a choirboy. Had he been with Tammy?

"This…thing ran in front of me and I screamed," Cassie told Claire. "The lovely elderly couple in the cart nearly had twin heart attacks!"

Claire waved a hand. "I'm sure you're exaggerating."

Cassie shook her head. "No. The thing came out of nowhere."

Claire laughed. "That's not what I meant! The folks from your tour are fine. Oliver's talking to them by the scale model right now."

That put Cassie's mind a little bit at ease, anyway. If anybody could get a bunch of people excited about Cypress, it was Oliver. He was one of those perky, peppy people who always seem to be happy wherever they were. He'd annoyed her for all of two seconds before she realized he was a sweet guy. He didn't hit on her either, since he clearly played for the other team.

"Thank God." She sank down into a chair at Tammy's table. "I didn't want Rick to know what a complete failure I am."

"You're not," Claire said as she sat beside her. "How long have you been here?"

"Too long. Nearly week. I started right after I nearly brought the Institute to a crashing halt."

"You have nothing on me, Cassie," Tammy said. "I've been here for years and I've seen it all. Except, apparently, whatever creature that was that ran you off the road."

Cassie had to smile. "I'll ask Ty. Maybe it's not poisonous. Or venomous." She shuddered. "Or rabid."

"That's it," Claire said with a smile. "Think positive."

Cassie clicked her tongue. "Never mind."

"Although you will get a chance to talk to Ty," Tammy said. "I'm almost jealous. That man is fine."

"Ty's little niece is adorable, isn't she Cassie?" Claire asked. "She came to Rick and Harmony's on Sunday."

"Yes, she is beautiful. A little doll." Cassie thought about how tense Ty had been before their latest round of lakeshore loving, as she was starting to think of their tangles in the tent-cabin. He'd never ended up talking about what had him so wound up before, though. Maybe she'd made him forget about it for a while.

"He's really good with her," Claire said.

"Oh yeah, the kid." Tammy gave a dramatic shiver. "I forgot he's got a niece. Watches her every weekend, too."

"Not into children, Tammy?" Claire teased.

"Not in the least. I don't care how fine the man is. If he comes with kids, I'm keeping far away."

Cassie shouldn't have cared about the pretty brunette's possible hots for Ty but now any worry was swept aside by Claire's input. And by the sparkle in her sister-in-law's eyes, that wasn't an accident. More matchmaking coming from the Chapman camp, huh? She'd seen the speculation on Harmony's face when she'd left the house with him Sunday night, although Rick had seemed a little less enthusiastic.

Cassie hid her smile. If they only knew just what Ty and Cassie were getting up to after the sun went down.

"You know Jake and I are trying," Claire said. "For a baby."

"Oh, that's wonderful!" Cassie put her hand over Claire's.

"Your kid will be gorgeous. I just know it."

"That's for sure," Tammy said. "Rick's son is a real cutie. And I can almost stand to be around him, now that he's past the drooling stage."

"I'm pretty sure he passed that stage a couple years ago," Claire said.

Claire talked about something Nick said the other day and Tammy laughed. Cassie only half-listened. She picked at the plastic ring around the top of her water bottle. Talking about kids, and about trying for babies, was something she'd never done. Not with the people she used to hang around with. She felt like she had nothing to contribute, aside from her genuine hope that Jake and Claire would be blessed and soon. Their baby really would be a knockout and the two of them would make fantastic parents.

"I really have to think about another job," Cassie said at last.

Claire turned to her. "Why?"

"Because I suck at this one, Claire."

As she watched she could see Claire's gifted mind going to work on the puzzle of Cassie's future employment. She might not know this sister-in-law very well but she knew the woman had smarts to spare. And when Claire tilted her head that certain way, it meant she was thinking.

"Maybe Jake can use your help out at the adventure courses?"

"What, like rock climbing?" Cassie asked. "Oh, I don't know."

"Yikes," Tammy said. "Not for me, thanks."

"I suppose I can hand out gear or something." She blew out a breath. "Maybe I'll go work at the coffee shop."

"Have you done that before?" Claire asked.

"I've never had a job," Cassie answered.

The other two women stared for a beat, and then Tammy shrugged. "If you work there maybe you can give Claire a discount on her beloved lattes."

Claire sighed out loud. "It'll have to be soon, then. No caffeine once I'm expecting."

"Expect a downturn in profits at the coffee shop," Tammy said.

Cassie laughed. She liked hanging around with these women. She'd never really had close girlfriends, just other bored rich girls with nothing better to do. First Harmony and Claire and now Tammy? Maybe she should try more of this connecting stuff. She'd certainly been rewarded by taking a couple of cracks at it with Ty.

"Speak of the devil."

Tammy's words brought Cassie's head up. Ty stood in the doorway of the break room. Her breath caught.

He looked delectable. His Henley shirt had the Cypress Institute logo she'd seen all over Harmony's clothes and his khaki cargo pants hung just right off his narrow hips. Sun brightened his cheeks and the tip of his nose and his eyes looked bright.

"Hey, Cassie."

God, was there anything sexier than Ty's voice saying her name?

Tammy and Claire stood, exchanging a look as they left the break room. Cassie could guess what they were up to.

"See you, Ty," Tammy said as she passed him. "Oh, Cassie needs to ask you something."

Ty arched a brow and Cassie glanced away. She drank more of her water and hoped her cheeks weren't as pink as they felt.

Jeez, maybe having girlfriends was overrated.

***

Claire grinned and Tammy winked as they left. When Ty looked back at Cassie she was staring holes into the tabletop.

She looked a little mussed, just like he'd been picturing her at the Institute's reception desk that morning. Maybe this job wasn't going as well as she might have hoped, either.

"What's up?"

She finally looked up at him. "Hmm?"

He set his tablet down on the table then turned one of the chairs around and straddled it. "What do you need to ask me?"

She rolled her eyes. "Jeez. Okay, there was this animal thing that ran in front of my cart today. I sort of swerved."

"You swerved?"

"Swerved. Ran off the path. Whatever."

He laughed.

"Oh, that's nice. Kick a girl when she's down."

Ty held up a hand. "I'm sorry. Are you okay?"

"Now?" She blew a loose strand of hair off her forehead. "I'm fine. And, thank God, the people I frightened nearly to death are fine too."

"Were they on the path?"

"No." She snorted. "Wise guy. They were in the cart with me. When I screamed they were a little…startled."

He managed to only grin this time. "That's too bad, but everyone's okay. Right?"

"So you're one of those 'let's look at the positive' people, too?"

He shrugged. "I guess." He folded his arms on the back of the chair. "So what did you want to ask me?"

"I just wondered if you could tell me what kind of beast that was."

"A beast, huh? Describe it?"

She held her hands out in front of her, about two feet apart. "It was this long. Furry. Big, fluffy tail."

"What color was it?"

"Brown. I think. It had a black head, though. What kind of freak animals do you have down here?"

He chuckled. "It was probably a fox squirrel."

She looked at him evenly. "Like that's a thing."

"I swear it is." He picked up his tablet and tapped the screen until he pulled up a picture of a fox squirrel on the Internet. "Here." He spun the table to face her. "See?"

She looked at it, and then shrugged.

"I guess it did look like that thing." She sighed and sat back. "It doesn't matter. It doesn't matter if it was a fox squirrel or a pig dog. It's no excuse."

"Excuse for what?"

"For losing it, Ty. My brother stuck his neck out, getting me a job. First Harmony and now Rick? I'm the mess that keeps on giving."

"You're not a mess." He reached out and covered her hand with his. "Your family doesn't think of you as a mess. Believe me."

"So you said the other night."

Ah, the other night. When she'd driven him crazy and then even further. "We never really had our talk."

Her eyes darted to the doorway of the break room, and then back to him. "Shh. I don't want everyone here to know what happened the other night."

"I promised you wouldn't be the subject of gossip, Cassie. You can believe me."

"I know."

Her simply-spoken statement said a lot more to him, though. She trusted him. For some reason that escaped him right then, she trusted him.

"So just get back up on the horse."

Her eyes went wide. "I have to ride a horse now?"

"No. Actually, I wanted to invite you to take one of my eco-tours tomorrow."

149

"Tomorrow?"

She nibbled on her full lower lip and he couldn't help but remember how sweet her kisses were.

Refocusing, he nodded. "Dr. Robbins thought it would be good for you."

"But what about Rick? Doesn't he need me here?"

"I already talked to Rick and he gave his okay."

"Big surprise there." She gave him a small smile. "I'm sure he's really going to miss me here."

Ty just shrugged. "So the tour is first thing. Right at nine."

"Okay."

She didn't look very okay, though.

He came to his feet. "And I promise, no pig dogs."

That earned him a laugh at least. She still looked worried, though.

"I have to find something else though, Ty. No joke."

He had no idea what to say to her now. He'd always tried to tell his sister Tracy what to do and look how good that had turned out?

Cassie was staring ahead, her mind most likely working as she tried to reason out her dilemma. God, he wanted to fix this for her. He was in no position for that, though. She had two brothers to look after her. What was he to her anyway? A guy she'd fooled around with a couple of times?

"Well, I'll see you in the morning," he said.

She nodded absently and he left the Sales Center. He felt unsettled and he was damned if he could figure out why.

Chapter 11

Ty found Cassie waiting for him in lobby of the Sales
Center Tuesday morning. She was turned away from him,
thumbing through the activity and property pamphlets set in
clear plastic holders on one of the low tables. He took a minute
to just check her out. Closely. Her shorts hugged her sweet ass
and her legs looked strong and sleek all the way down to her
sneakered feet. He'd felt the strength in those slender legs. In her
smoothly muscled arms, too. She'd nearly pulled the iron
headboard off his bed when he'd driven her crazy the other
night. And after? Mmm.

He must have made a sound, he wasn't sure, because she
straightened and turned to face him. Harmony must have loaned
her that Cypress Institute shirt but he couldn't imagine it
hugging any other woman's body but Cassie's. Damn.

"Good morning," she said.

"Hey." Brilliant conversationalist, Ty. "Good morning. All
set for an adventure?"

She arched one graceful brow. "You promised me I
wouldn't have to ride a horse."

"And you don't. We'll be taking the gator."

Her mouth dropped open. "A gator?"

He smiled. "It's a rugged kind of golf cart, Cassie."

"Oh, one of those green and yellow ones? I saw those in the parking lot."

"Yep. No worries."

"Yeah. For you."

"And you. I promised you we'd tour the tamer parts of Cypress today."

She didn't look too reassured but she nodded. "I'll take your word for it. How many people are you touring today?"

"Just you and two ladies from the conservation club."

She smiled. "Is one of those ladies Lettie?"

He laughed. "God, no. I love her and she's a great friend to my mother but the woman wears me out."

"I like her, too. She's feisty."

Her eyes sparkled and he almost forgot what they were talking about. Seriously. Just then, the ladies from the conservation club entered the Sales Center.

"Let's head out, then." He turned to face the two women, ladies about the same age as his mother. One was tall and thin. She had a long gray-streaked braid resting over one shoulder and wore some flowy shirt with embroidered jeans and Birkenstock sandals. The other was a little bit stockier, with very short salt-

and-pepper hair. She wore olive green overalls, work boots and a no-nonsense expression.

"Ty Walsh?" the shorter one asked. When he nodded, she stuck out her hand toward him. "I'm Marge Atkins."

Ty shook her outstretched hand. "Very nice to meet you, Marge."

"And I'm Marigold Atkins." The taller woman smiled. "We're sisters."

Ty marveled at that for second, and then shook her hand too. "It's a pleasure to meet both of you. Cassie Chapman will be joining us."

At the mention of her name, Cassie came forward and shook hands with the ladies. Her smile was genuine and both Marge and Marigold quickly fell under her spell.

"Miss Chapman!" Marigold grasped Cassie's hand in both of hers. "I'd heard you were giving property tours for the Sales Center."

"I was, yes."

"But I thought you were working at the Institute?" Marge put in.

Cassie gave a nod. "Yes, I was there as well."

"A true Renaissance woman?" Marigold asked with a grin.

"More like Jack of all trades, master of none."

Both ladies crinkled their brows, and then laughed when Cassie waved her own comment away. Ty didn't miss it, though. Cassie really believed there was nothing she could do well.

"Why don't we head out?" he offered.

Marge gave a firm nod and strode toward the door. Marigold trailed after her, chattering about the possible animals they would see on the tour while her sister spoke of taking a closer look at the prevalence of weeds choking the lakes and retention ponds.

"After you?" he asked Cassie.

At her nod he placed his hand on her lower back, his fingers tingling where they touched her. Withdrawing, he stepped back and simply watched her head out after the Atkins sisters. Saying a silent prayer that he'd be able to concentrate on the tour, he stepped outside to join them. Cassie might not know if he misrepresents any animals or plants they encounter but Marge and Marigold? He was afraid they'd school him but good if he screwed up.

The gator cart was a custom four-seater. As he'd expected, the sisters took the rear seats, leaving Cassie to sit beside him. He had access to a larger, six-seater as well, which he used when he had tours from the high school. He liked running the more intimate tours, though. For where they were going, a small group was always easier to keep on the quiet side of things. However, with Cassie seated so close and the growing heat of the day sending her flowery-sweet scent his way, he was going to have a tough time for sure.

"Today we're going to tour the east side of the property," he began. "Not too far into the wild, though."

Cassie looked relieved and he didn't hear any complaints from the sisters. As they left the manicured paths lining the golf course, Ty went on to point out the water fowl and birds of prey as he caught sight of them.

"I'd heard that homes with alternative energy sources will be built soon?" Marge asked.

"Yes!" Marigold said. "Solar and wind, perhaps?"

"What, windmills?" Cassie asked.

"Turbines, dear," Marigold put in. "There is plenty of property to put them, isn't there Mr. Walsh?"

"There is, but the sounds can be intrusive," Ty said. "I believe algae fields would be better suited to the land and its inhabitants."

"Yes, algae," Marge said. "Nice, clean fuel. Do you know

when construction would begin on the fields?"

"When will the houses be converted to use the energy?" Marigold asked.

Ty just shook his head as he maneuvered the cart down the sandy path. "That's something the Institute and the developers are working on. I don't know the particulars at this point. I am excited about the prospect, though."

"Algae, huh?" Cassie shrugged. "I guess that would be very green."

Ty threw her a smile as Marge and Marigold laughed from the rear.

"I know they're looking at builders who specialize in eco-friendly energy," Ty said. "Like they did with some of the solar homes, everyone would be able to convert if they want to. Once it's in place, of course."

"So where did you put that alligator?" Cassie asked.

"What alligator?" Marigold asked.

Cassie turned to face the sisters. "Mr. Walsh helped my brother Jake when an alligator insisted on trying out the adventure courses."

Marigold laughed again. "The adventure courses? Oh, I wish I was brave enough to try them."

157

"It's just running and swimming, Marigold," Marge said. "I've done the circuit that equals a half-marathon several times."

This didn't surprise Ty in the least. He reasoned that Marge could run circles around Jake if given half the chance, not to mention around himself.

"I've seen you out at the courses too, Mr. Walsh," Marge went on. "Very impressive."

Cassie shifted and Ty could almost feel her watching him.

"Impressive, huh?" she asked.

"Oh, yes," Marigold said. "Marge told me he could vault over the obstacles as fast as Jake Chapman."

Cassie clicked her tongue. "You've been holding out on me."

Ty shrugged. "Maybe I'll get you up on the climbing wall, Cassie. Show you some pointers?"

"Pointers? Where to place my hands, you mean?"

He chuckled and then coughed to cover up his reaction. He knew he was playing with fire but it was fun to tease her, and not just when they were alone in the tent-cabin.

"I wouldn't mind some pointers myself," Marigold said. "Why, just the other day Lettie was talking about your physical prowess."

"Prowess?" Marge asked. "With what?"

"Hmm, I'm not sure," Marigold answered. "Something about the stamina of a young man needing to find an outlet."

Cassie stiffened, and then turned with a jerk to face forward. Ty just nodded and changed the subject.

Luckily, the sisters were only too able to fill the silence as more of the wild property revealed itself. By the time he'd reached the far end of his planned route and turned back, he was more than ready to deposit the three of them safely back at the Sales Center. Then he belatedly noticed that his tent-cabin was visible from this side of the path.

"What's that little shelter?" Marigold asked. "And what is it doing all the way out here?"

"That's Ty's tent-cabin, Marigold," Marge said. "You stay out here often, Mr. Walsh?"

"Often enough," Ty answered.

"It's very remote," Marigold observed. "What on earth do you do to occupy yourself?"

Ty nearly swallowed his tongue. "I do okay," he managed to say.

He heard a soft snicker from Cassie's direction. "I bet you do all kinds of okay."

Her comment got another round of laughter from the sisters. God, if he was playing with fire Cassie was holding the matches. Talk turned back to the scenery and habitats, and Ty felt the ground grow a bit more steady beneath the nubby tires of the gator. What was it about this girl that put him so off balance?

When he risked a glance at her, he knew just what she was thinking. Would she want to come back here with him tonight? There was unfinished business between them after all. Sure, they'd given a lot to each other last time but Ty wanted more. More sex, sure. But more Cassie.

And tonight, he hoped to have her.

***

Cassie smoothed her damp palms over her borrowed khaki shorts as she sat in the courtyard of the coffee shop. Harmony had given her one of her cast-off Institute T-shirts, too. It was soft as silk and obviously worn to within an inch of its life. The sage green color was pretty but she felt like she was wearing a costume. The Keds were her own, along with the pretty underwear that felt like her only links to her past life. After the wild and rugged tour she'd taken this morning? This was so far from laying out on the beach in Monte Carlo. That was for sure.

Not to mention how she'd felt when Ty's gaze had fallen on

her again and again throughout the tour. They might have been the only two people in that funny cart-truck thing, considering the heat zinging between them. Although maybe the Atkins sisters figured something out, too. When Ty returned to the Sales Center, they'd both looked at her like they were dying to ask just what Ty got up to out at the far lakeshore. No way was she going to open up to those two. Although very different they both seemed sweet. Still, they palled around with Lettie. That woman thrived on gossip and she was very good friends with Ty's mother. Two very good reasons for Cassie to keep her mouth shut.

As if on cue, Lettie lifted her glass of iced tea in Cassie's direction. She returned the gesture with her bottle of sparkling water, and then sighed. Life in the fish bowl that was Cypress Corners. Still, not a tabloid reporter in sight.

She looked at the Sales Center across the street, relieved that she didn't have to give a tour today. She really wasn't good at it. It wasn't that she couldn't remember all the key points Rick had drilled into her head. She just found it didn't interest her. Rick had told her to take the day off after the tour with Ty, for whatever reason. He'd told her to go grab a cup of coffee too, which was weird.

"Hey, sis!" Jake called, raising a hand.

Suddenly Rick's insistence made sense. Another set up, not that she could imagine what part Jake would play in it.

"Hi, Jake. What's up?"

Jake nodded a greeting to Lettie, and then sat at Cassie's table. "Cass, I need to ask you a favor."

She crossed her arms and leaned back. "Oh? Rick put you up to this?"

Jake's eyes widened but she knew he was faking. "Put me up to what?"

"You can't shit a shitter, Jake. Tell me what's up and I won't be forced to hurt you."

Jake laughed. "Damn, I'd forgotten how sharp you are." He rubbed the middle of his chest. "I remember you could punch pretty hard for a girl, too."

"So tell me."

"I'd like you to come work for me at the adventure courses."

"Doing what?"

"Handing out equipment. Having people sign the waivers before participating. Making sure the fridge is stocked with drinks and the counters with power bars. That kind of stuff."

She thought for a minute, and then nodded. "I know you

guys have all gone out on a limb to find me someplace to work. Harmony and Rick have already done their best so you're up next."

Jake leaned forward. "We want you to stay here, Cassie. I know I love having you here."

She blinked away the tears that suddenly filled her vision. "I like being here but I don't belong."

"Why the hell not?" He looked around, and then lowered his voice. "Why not? Your family is here. Not in Europe and certainly not in Boston."

She acknowledged his words with a shrug. "But I don't have a place, Jake. I don't fit in."

He studied her, her face solemn. "This isn't about work."

It wasn't a question and they both knew the answer anyway. "I have to figure out what the hell I'm going to do with the rest of my life."

"Are you quoting Bill? Give me a break."

"He's right though, isn't he?"

"No, he's not. Listen, I'm glad he sent you down here. It's been great just knowing you're close by. Seeing you almost every day."

"Family stuff." He nodded and she felt the love coming

from him and smiled. "Claire told me you're trying for a baby."

A grin spread across Jake's face. "Yeah. It's a tough job but I'm up to it."

She punched him in the arm. "All right, all right."

Something caught Jake's eye and she followed his gaze to see Rick crossing the street toward them. An uneasy feeling skittered over her.

"Is this an intervention?" she asked.

Jake laughed and waved Rick over. "No. Do you need one?"

"Nope. Not in the market for one, anyway."

"Hey there," Rick said. "I hear you're going to work for Jake?"

She smirked at Jake, and then faced Rick again. "Looks like it."

Rick grinned.

"You don't have to look so giddy about it. Isn't enough that you pawned me off on Ty this morning?"

"I'm sure he was happy to take you." He seemed to catch his own words and scowled. "That's not that I meant."

Laughing at his distress, she waved a hand. "Lighten up, Rick. I didn't think you meant anything by that."

Rick looked relieved but it was Jake who nudged her with

his elbow.

"You're seeing him, though?" Jake asked.

She bit her lip, unsure of just what to tell her big brothers. "We've been talking."

Jake slanted her a look. "Talking?"

She bristled. "I'm not getting into this with either of you."

"Cass, you're a big girl," Rick said. "I'm not going to tell you what to do."

"Then why do I feel like you are?"

He shrugged. "I just don't want you to get hurt."

"Like you said, I'm a big girl. If Dad thinks I can get along down here, shouldn't that be reason enough to let me make my own decisions?"

He rubbed the back of his neck. "Speaking of Bill, he's been emailing me."

Jake cursed. "He's always emailing you. The question is, are you answering him?"

"No. But he's been asking about you, Cassie. Has he called or texted you?"

"Nope," she said. "And I like it that way."

"I hear you," Rick said. "You do know he's due for a visit in two weeks. He's coming down Memorial Day weekend."

"In two weeks?" Cassie did the math in her head. That would be almost a month to the day since her exile. "Why?"

"Meeting with investors before the summer heat moves in." He lifted his chin toward Jake. "They want to see the additions to your course and discuss the new alternative energy incentives with me."

"Two weeks," she said again. "Tell you what, I'm not going to worry about him now."

Rick shook his head. "You haven't been here for one of his visits, Cassie. He swoops in with his usual bluster like a hurricane."

"He's an energy vampire, sis," Jake put in. "Just sucks the life out of you."

"He can't do anything else to me, guys. He cut me off. He sent me away." Her throat tightened but she wouldn't shed any tears for Bill Chapman. Not in front of her brothers. "He washed his hands of me."

"If you say so," Rick said. "Just be on your guard."

"Yeah," Jake added. "No one can get to you like Bill."

"I know." She pushed her hair back off her face. "I don't have a place, Rick. I'm on borrowed time. I know that."

Rick's eyes softened. "You always have a place here,

Cassie."

It was just about the same thing Jake said and it really affected her. Tears pricked at her eyes again but she just nodded. "Thanks." Even if she didn't believe either of them, the sentiment still made her heart swell a little bit.

Rick apparently took his lead from her and dragged the subject away from their father. "Now, about Ty."

"Oh, don't you start," she said.

Rick shrugged and came to his feet. "I'm going to see if I can steal my wife away to grab some lunch. See you later?"

It was a question and she knew what he was getting at. It was about Ty again.

She smirked at him and he laughed softly. Jake laughed too and grabbed her bottle to take a sip. She liked hanging with her brothers. She might not have a place but she sure felt good around them. With Claire and Harmony and even Tammy. And then there was Ty.

Would he ask her to make good on all that innuendo she tossed his way during that tour? She grabbed her bottle back from Jake.

A girl could hope.

Chapter 12

Ty walked out of the Institute and saw Cassie sitting with Jake. She laughed at something her brother said, tossing her head back. She looked so pretty and relaxed in that moment his stomach clenched. He really should figure out a way to get rid of that tension that always seemed to cling to her. Almost always, anyway. She'd seemed pretty relaxed once he pleased her a couple of times. Jeez, was he going to start beating his chest now?

"Hey, Chapmans," he said with a wave as he stepped up to their table.

"Hi, Ty," Cassie said, a smile still playing on her lips.

"Hey, Ty." Jake eyed his sister with an expectant look on his face. "You gonna tell him, sis?"

"Tell me what?" Ty sat down and leaned his arms on the table. "Don't tell me another critter ran you off the road. I thought you weren't giving tours anymore."

She rolled her eyes, looking adorably put out. "It didn't and I'm not. Jake is all puffed up because he swooped in and pulled my butt out of the fire."

"Not a fire, exactly," Jake said. "Cassie's going to come work for me at the adventure courses."

"Yeah?" Ty grinned. "Maybe you can spot me."

Cassie's eyes rounded for a second but Ty managed to keep his expression even. What was he doing, teasing her in front of one of her brothers?

"I'm going to be working in the shed, Ty. Unless you plan on extreme shopping and form signing, I think you'll be okay on your own."

Ty chuckled and leaned back. "Okay. Do you start tomorrow?"

She sighed. "I suppose. My new boss takes the title to a new level."

"Hardly," Jake said. "I'm easy. Just ask Claire."

"Not touching that one," Cassie said.

Ty saw the spark of family connection between them, and it seemed even stronger than it had been at the picnic. She was feeling more at ease around them and it looked good on her.

"I plan to run the course tomorrow afternoon," Ty said. "I'll see you there."

She nodded. "Jake's going to show me the ropes. Literally."

"And harnesses, sis. You need to know the safety stuff, too."

"Why?" she asked.

"Because you're going to be answering questions when

people come to the shed. Don't worry. There are notes you can refer to."

"Great. More notes. Maybe I'll go work for Ty."

"Doing what?" Jake held up his hand. "Never mind. I don't want to know."

Ty just stared at them for a beat. Did Jake know he and Cassie were…whatever it was they were doing?

"Look what you're doing to Ty," Cassie said with a mock-scowl. "You're going to scare him away."

"I don't think you'd like working for me anyway," Ty said. "Lots of critters. Not to mention bugs and snakes and gators."

She held up both hands. "'Nuff said, man. I believe you. The relative safety of the shed will be fine, thanks."

Jake stood, stretching his arms over his head. "I'm going to head over to the swim club. Are you finished Ty, or do you have another tour this afternoon?"

"Nope. I'm done."

"Then why don't you come? Maybe Cassie can join us?"

"Swimming in April?"

"The water is geothermally heated," Ty said automatically. "Very comfortable."

"Even so, I think I'll pass. You can go, Ty. You don't have

to keep me company, you know."

"I was just going to get myself a drink."

"Then I'll leave you two kids to your malted." Jake winked and grabbed her bottle of water. "Get two straws, Ty."

Cassie punched her brother in the arm and Jake feigned injury. It reminded Ty of the time before his dad died. When he and Tracy could kid around with each other. He missed that. He missed her, too. Even a messed-up Tracy was better than no Tracy at all.

"Hey, where'd you go?" Cassie asked.

Ty glanced over to find her watching him closely. He mentally shook himself and managed a smile. "Just thinking about brothers and sisters."

Her lips parted, and then she shook her head. "I'm not going to pry."

"You're not prying. We're friends, Cassie. You can ask me anything."

"You're thinking about your sister, aren't you?"

Ty nodded. "She's been gone over two years and I still miss her."

"Sure. When I think of all the time I wasted running away from my family it makes me feel all twisted up inside."

He cocked a brow at her. "Are we finally having the talk we never got around to Sunday night?"

She smiled, her cheeks turning a little pink. "Maybe. Although I think a rain check is in order."

"Yeah?"

She gestured around the populated courtyard and shrugged. "Lots of ears around here."

"True. I have nothing to hide, though."

"Maybe *you* don't."

"Then come to dinner with me tonight. We can go to the Boathouse. Excellent seafood."

"And then maybe a trip to your tent-cabin?" she asked softly.

Her voice caressed him in all the best ways. He gave a short nod and she smiled.

"Okay, then. You can pick me up at Rick and Harmony's."

"Six okay?"

"Sure. That will give us lots of time to talk."

He was glad there was a table between them because the look in her eyes told him she wasn't thinking about talking right now. And neither was he. Just the thought of what they could share tonight made him want to grab her right now.

172

"Cassie, dear." His mother walked up to the table, a bright smile on her face. "Isn't this nice?"

"Hello, Mrs. Walsh," Cassie said. "How are you?"

"I'm just fine." She turned to him. "Ty, aren't you going to say hello to your mother?"

"Hello, Mom. What are you up to this afternoon?"

"Nothing too strenuous, believe me. Nothing to worry about."

"Here, Mrs. Walsh." Cassie stood. "Take my seat."

"Now, aren't you sweet?" His mother sat. "Thank you, Cassie."

Cassie turned to him. "Ty, um. I guess I'll see you later?"

"I'll see you at six," he said.

She made her way over to the Sales Center, probably happy for the escape. His mother looked like she was plotting something and he could probably guess just what was on her mind.

"Say it," he said when it was just the two of them.

"Say what?" she asked, all innocence.

"Say what you want to say about me and Cassie."

"Then there is a you-and-Cassie?" Her eyes twinkled. "I knew it!"

"All right, fine. I'm taking her to dinner tonight. So I guess that means we're dating."

"Hmm. Dinner. Not just another romp out at your love shack?"

"Jeez, Mom. Will you quit it?"

She grinned at him. Actually grinned. "When you blush you look just like you did when you were a little boy."

Ty rolled his eyes. "Did you want a latte or a sweet tea, Mom?" He stood. "I'm just about to get myself something."

"Hmm. Maybe one of those blended ice things. It's getting warm out here."

Ty just nodded and went into the coffee shop. Lettie caught his eye as he passed, and that woman had the same glint in her eye as his mother did. Great. He had to make sure nothing got around about Cassie. The last thing she needed to worry about was more gossip. Wasn't that what brought her to Cypress in the first place?

He couldn't help but be grateful for the tabloid reporters, as slimy as they could be. If it weren't for them, he never would have met her.

***

"Where is he taking you?" Harmony asked as she searched

for something to lend Cassie.

"The Boathouse."

Harmony's face lit. "I took Rick there for our first date!
Well, it wasn't really a date but he did eat gator for the first time
that night."

Cassie shivered. "Gator? What is with this place?"

"They have other things too, Cassie. Shrimp po'boys and
oysters and steaks and burgers. I think you'll like it."

"What's it like? Fancy?"

"God, no. Jeans and a pretty top should work." Harmony
turned back to her closet. "I have some shirts my mom gave
me." She pulled out a gorgeous turquoise top of gauzy material.
"Here. The stuff she gives me is always on the bohemian side of
things."

Cassie took the blouse. It was soft and sheer. "This is
beautiful. Thank you." She set it on the bed. "I haven't met your
parents, Harmony. I though they lived here."

"They run the Recreation Café out on the nature trails most
of the year. They live in their RV, though. In fact, they've been
up in Orlando for the past couple of weeks."

Cassie nodded. "I wondered why they weren't at the
picnic."

"My dad gets wanderlust now and then and he leaves the kids he trained in charge of the place."

"Hmm. Maybe after I destroy Jake's faith in me I can go work for your father."

Harmony's brow furrowed. "Don't say that. Your brothers are not going to lose faith in you."

Cassie sat down on the bed. "I'm a screw up. I always have been. Only now my poor brothers have to clean up my messes."

"They love you. I can see that. Why can't you?"

Cassie thought for a minute. She did feel the affection from them. Even Rick was more open around her than he'd ever been.

"I do see it. I'm just afraid that when I leave, things will go back to the way they were."

"You're leaving?"

"Aren't I? I don't want to overstay my welcome."

"You couldn't." Harmony sat beside her and wrapped her in a hug. "You're the sister I never had, Cassie. I love having you here."

"Even after I left the Institute a mess?"

Harmony waved a hand. "Mess, shmess. Becky got a handle on things as soon as she got back." She smiled. "No lasting damage."

"That's good." Cassie blew out a breath. "I just feel like I'm drifting. Just like Bill said."

Now Harmony looked pissed. "Don't get me started on your father, Cassie. He's selfish and controlling and you don't need that in your life. Not when you're trying to figuring things out."

"My God, you get me." Cassie smiled. "I'm so glad my brother found you."

Harmony shrugged. "It was mutual. We butted heads and then fell in love."

"Just like that, huh? Sounds too easy."

"It wasn't easy at all." Harmony laughed. "But nothing worth having is easy."

"Are you asking about me and Ty? Subtle."

"Hey, subtlety isn't my thing. I work with plants, Cassie. There's no innuendo or tiptoeing around. They're either thriving or not."

"Easier to figure out than people, I bet."

"Way easier. But I see something between you and Ty. And not just heat."

"Heat?" Cassie thought of the look he'd given her across that table this afternoon. "Yeah, there's that."

"He's a good guy. He has a lot on his plate, though."

"His niece and visitation. I get it."

"You know about that?"

"I know he wants Riley more than they get her. We haven't talked too much about it, though."

"You should take a boat ride with him. Get him out on the water and just watch him open up."

"He's a real nature boy. That's true."

"Or maybe just get him out to the tent-cabin?"

Cassie stared at her. "You know."

"Yes, I know. We all know."

She clutched at her heart. "I'm so sorry, Harmony. I didn't mean to bring my mess down here."

"What mess?"

"Gossip. It can get pretty nasty."

"No one is gossiping. Not about you and Ty, anyway. I just meant the family knows. Your brothers and me and Claire. That's all."

"Tammy thinks something's up, too."

"Oh, Tammy always thinks something's up. You watch. One of these days she's going to fool around and fall in love herself."

Cassie doubted the woman would give a guy the chance at

her heart, but maybe Harmony was right. She knew Tammy much better than Cassie did.

"Maybe she's just a Lettie in training," Cassie said.

Harmony gave a dramatic shudder. "Save us from another Lettie!"

They shared a laugh and Cassie felt that connection again. She would miss it when she left. But she would leave. That was never in question. She'd prove herself to her father and get back to her life. And all of this in Cypress? The warmth and the lake. Her family and Ty. It would all make for nice memories.

She was determined to make a few more memories tonight, though. With Ty.

Chapter 13

Ty picked her up at six on the dot. She smiled as she walked to the front door. He had told her he was a boy scout. She opened the door and took a long minute to just drink him in. He wore oxfords and khakis and one of those Henley shirts she just loved on him. It hugged his upper body just enough to show her the fine build she knew was underneath.

"Hey," she said.

He ran his gaze over her. Harmony's top was a little snug across her breasts but the color was so pretty and it grazed the top of her jeans. It was a good thing Harmony had filled her in on the place, or she would have been way overdressed if she'd worn any of the outfits she'd brought with her. When she thought about it, she hadn't touched much of the stuff in her luggage since she'd been here.

"You look nice," he said with a grin. "Casual suits you."

"Casual, huh?"

They shared a smile. They both knew he'd seen her in way fewer clothes than this.

"I'll see you guys later," she called into the family room.

Rick and Harmony made some sound of agreement and Cassie stepped out onto the porch. The air was still warm and the scent of orange blossoms was heavy.

"Wow, that smells good."

"The wind shifted. There are orange groves just south of Cypress."

"Okay, nature boy." She went up on her toes and placed her nose right in the hollow of his throat. "Mmm, you smell good too."

He flicked a glance toward the house, and then took her mouth in a kiss. He tasted as good as he smelled and she wrapped her arms around his neck. When his hands cupped her butt, she leaned back with a grin.

"Getting ahead of ourselves, are we?"

He shook his head at her. "You're the one who did that sniff thing you do. It drives me crazy."

"Sniff thing? I've done that before?"

"When you cuddle close you do."

She bit her lower lip. "I don't know if I should be flattered or embarrassed right now."

"Flattered, believe me." He released her and waved her ahead of him. "Let's go before I forget my manners."

Smiling like an idiot, she hurried to his truck. He opened the door for her, of course. He always did. She slid into the seat and waited for him.

He got in and started the truck. "We're going to take the perimeter road around the lake. The Boathouse isn't technically on Cypress property but it's a favorite with residents. Lots of townies, too."

After about ten minutes he took a turn-off to the right. They followed a winding road, which led through the woody growth toward what looked like little more than a sprawling shack by the lakeside.

He stopped the truck next to a big beat-up SUV and turned to her. "Here we are."

"This is The Boathouse?"

"Yep."

The restaurant boasted a lone dock to the rear with a few small boats tethered to it. But lights shone inside the shack and she could hear music on the warm air as she stepped out of the truck.

The Boathouse was loud and crowded and filled with wooden picnic tables.

"This looks like a fun place," she said.

"It is. The food's delicious, too."

They greeted the hostess, who showed them to a table near

the wide screened windows. Ty sat on a bench across from Cassie. It felt like they were still outside; the chirps and croaks of whatever lived in the woods were loud through the screens.

"It's a little primitive, huh?"

Ty nodded. "Do you like it?"

She smiled. "I'm finding I like getting back to nature."

He growled softly at her. "A beer okay?"

"Sure."

A server stopped by their table and Ty ordered their drinks.

"And an order of gator tail," he said.

She waited until the server left to slant him a look. "Gator? Harmony warned me about that."

"It's delicious."

"I'll take your word on that."

"The sauces are good, too. Sweet and hot." His hazel eyes sparkled. "Like you."

She flushed from his simple words. "Ty, you're magic with that tongue."

"I've been told that."

She couldn't help but remember just what he'd done with that tongue. He'd licked and sucked and kissed her all over.

"How quick is the service in this place?"

Ty just grinned as the server brought them their beers and plates.

It turned out the sauces were very yummy but she still wouldn't try the gator. The catfish was delicious, though. And something she'd never had before. As they shared a dessert of the best key lime pie she'd ever tasted, she thought about what Harmony said. Was she putting down roots here? Did she want to?

"So what do you think?" Ty asked her.

"I like this place, Ty. I'd come again."

His brows arched and she laughed.

"Stop that. You're a naughty boy. I'm going to tell your mother."

"Please, don't," he groaned. "Did I tell you she calls the tent-cabin my love shack?"

"Seriously? Wait. You've had women out there before. Of course you have. You're not a choirboy."

"I haven't, Cassie. Not until you."

"So it's my love shack, too." She grinned now. "Then let's get going."

***

Ty felt like his skin was too tight. Just a few words from

her, given with just the right look, sent him into overdrive. He couldn't pay the check fast enough. She stood there by the table as he scribbled his signature across the slip, looking so good in her tight jeans and pretty top. All through dinner he'd caught glimpses through that peekaboo shirt. The shadow of her bra strap. A hint of cleavage. Even her delicate collar bones looked sexy in that shirt with the dim lighting at the Boathouse. She was right. They would definitely come here again.

"Come on," he said, trying to keep the urgency out of his voice.

He managed to keep to the road as he made his way to the tent-cabin. When they got there he shut the engine off and turned toward her.

"Are you sure about this?" he asked.

He'd about die if she said she wasn't but he was a gentleman. He would never want to pressure her.

"Sure about what?" she asked, her eyes wide.

He snorted. "You know what, Cassie. I'm not going to take advantage."

She came closer, a small smile playing on her lips. "Come on, Ty. You know you can't take advantage of me if I'm taking advantage of you."

There was an edge to her words but with her fingers teasing his chest through the V in his shirt he was damned if he could figure it out right now. Instead, he crushed his mouth to hers.

She tasted like citrus from the pie and sugar from just being her. When she sucked on his tongue, his eyes nearly rolled back in his head. His dick grew so hard so fast he could hardly breathe.

Pulling back a bit, he cursed softly. "Ah, Cassie."

She put her hands on the sides of his head just the way he liked and nibbled on his lips. "Let's go inside the love shack."

His laugh came out as a groan when she put her hand on his crotch. Easing away from her, he opened the door and she slid over with him. The girl could move fast, which he saw when she took his hand and hurried toward the little wooden porch.

When they got inside he shut the door and pulled his shirt up and over his head. He felt like he was on fire and the sooner he got his clothes off and his body on hers he would begin to feel some relief.

"As much as I like that shirt you better take it off," he said, coming closer.

Her lips parted and she did as he said. "Anything you want."

"Anything?"

She began to shimmy out of her jeans as he toed off his shoes. Settling on the bed, she eyed his chest.

"You are so pretty," she said.

"Pretty?"

She nodded. "Yes. Those dimples. Those eyes. And that body."

It was his turn to shake his head. "I can hardly find the words to describe how beautiful you are, Cassie."

Delight was clear on her face and he knew it was the right thing to say. She'd probably been with enough bull-shitters to know one when she saw one. He sure wasn't one. Looking at her in her bra and panties, he had no reason to be.

He came closer, and then shoved his pants and boxer briefs to the floor. Dropping his pants next to the bed, he came up and over her. They kissed again, her arms wrapped around his neck as she made the most delicious noises.

"Ty." She nibbled on his neck. "Mmm, I love the way you feel against me."

He grunted something in agreement and undid the tiny hook at the front of her pretty pink bra. He'd only glimpsed her breasts before but, damn, they were the prettiest he'd ever seen. Round and pale and tipped with tight nipples a little bit darker than her lips.

"You're so beautiful, Cassie." He bent his head and licked one nipple. "So sweet."

She arched and he covered one breast with his hand as he suckled the other. The lace of her panties was wet when he touched her. Her flesh was scalding hot. He had to get inside her before he came all over her soft skin.

Reaching over the side of the bed, he grabbed his pants and searched the pocket for the condom he'd put there.

"You're prepared?" she asked, laughter in her voice.

Her eyes were bright as he stared down at her.

"Boy scout, remember?"

She smiled and he kissed her again. Her lips clung to his so sweetly when he pulled away. As he sheathed himself she slid off her little panties. When he looked down at her, primed and ready, he could just stare. She was completely naked now, and he couldn't imagine a sexier sight. Toned curves and smooth skin and a rosy flush he knew he put there. Without waiting another second, he slid all the way inside.

She cried out, her body arching as she took all of him. She was so tight he had to hold himself still before everything was over too fast. They might have kidded around about getting all hot and bothered in his truck but this was more intense than anything he'd experienced with any other girl back then. And nothing with any other woman since could compare to the way he felt when he was inside Cassie.

He moved inside her, fast and hard, and she began to moan. Bracing himself on his arms, he held himself off her as he rotated his hips with every thrust. He knew he touched every nerve inside her. He could feel her climbing higher and higher.

She clutched at him instead of the headboard tonight, her fingers wrapped around his biceps as she rose. When she came beneath him, sobbing his name, he nearly shouted his own climax. A few more thrusts and he joined her, feeling as though every bone and every muscle melted away as he sank down on top of her.

With his head on the pillow, he faced her. Her eyes were closed and she breathed through parted lips. His own breath was still coming fast as his heart hammered.

"You okay?" he managed to ask.

Her eyes opened and they were as dark as the midnight sky. "Oh, yeah. Ty Walsh, you have some impressive moves."

He withdrew gently and blew out a breath. "Cassie, you nearly made me come in my pants just kissing me in the truck. I was lucky to make it to the bed."

She turned to face him, her hands tucked under one cheek. "Then I must be lucky, too."

Turning onto his back, he held her close as she settled into the crook of his arm. Her head rested against his shoulder as she idly played her fingers over his chest. She felt as soft as anything he'd ever touched. Even her hair was like silk against his fingers. He sensed something was still bugging her, though. He'd caught glimpses of it before and he could almost hear her thoughts working.

"Do you want to have that talk now?" he asked.

She shifted to lean on one elbow and faced him. "I guess we should."

He studied her for a minute. Her hair was a mess of waves and her face was still flushed pink. Her eyes, though. Her eyes looked very solemn.

"Only if you want to talk," he said. "My crap will still be there, whether I talk about it or not."

"But your crap isn't just about yourself."

"And yours is?"

She blew out a breath. "Ty, my family has stuck their necks out for me so many times since I came here. I just keep disappointing them over and over. You could never disappoint your family."

He dragged his gaze away from her to collect his thoughts. "I abandoned my sister, Cassie. Maybe if I'd hung around after our dad died things would be different."

"Different, how?"

He brushed his hair back from his forehead and faced her again. "I don't know. Tracy was pretty wild even before I left for college. She must have been just too much for my mother to handle."

"I've met your mother, remember? She is very sweet but I'd bet she was as strict as she could be with your sister. Was she a pushover with you?"

"Not at all." He grinned. "She called me on every bit of crap I tried to get away with."

Cassie nodded. "And was she any different with your sister?"

"I guess not. Tracy was just wild. She always was."

A look flickered across Cassie's face before she looked away. "Like me."

He touched her chin and gently turned back to him. "You're not self-destructive like she was. You don't put yourself first before anybody else."

She blinked at him. "How do you know?"

He smiled. "You've told me how much you don't want to disappoint your family. Believe me, Tracy didn't give a shit about our feelings. It's a hard truth, but one I've had to face since she died."

"She died in a car accident?"

"Of her own making. She was drunk and wrapped her car around a telephone pole. I say a prayer of thanks every day that Riley wasn't in that car with her."

"Thank God." Cassie looked at him for so long he thought she wasn't going to say anything more. Then she sighed. "I've made a lot of mistakes, Ty."

"Who hasn't?"

"You."

He blew out a breath. "I told you before. I'm no saint."

"Choirboy, but I get it." She smiled but it was a little bit sad. "I've never cared about what anybody thought before."

"Yeah? What about your father?"

She frowned. "What about him?"

"You can't say you don't care about what he thinks."

"Maybe. I don't care if I disappoint him, though. His

opinion doesn't matter."

"But his attention does?"

"What do you mean?"

"Look, I've never met your father. I only know as much about him as your brothers share. He's a cold son-of-a-bitch who left your mother, right?"

"Yes. And he never paid us any real attention."

"Until the tabloids."

She nodded. "He sat up and took notice then. And not in a good way."

"Maybe it was in a good way."

She smirked at him. "Yeah?"

He wrapped his arms around her, bringing his face to hers. "It brought you here. To Cypress and to my bed."

That earned him the grin he'd been looking for.

"I can't argue with that," she said. "How about we put a pin in the rest of this talk. Did you bring another condom or was that the only one?"

"There's more in the nightstand." He turned to pin her beneath him. "I made sure to stock up."

"Pretty confident."

"I know what I want." He kissed the sweet skin at the side

of her neck. "And I'm pretty sure I know what you want, too."

When he moved down her body, he knew he'd give them both what they wanted.

At least for now.

Chapter 14

"These harnesses are all tangled," Cassie said, leaning her hands on the counter.

Jake lifted his head from his tablet to stare at her. "So untangle them."

She blew a hair out of her eyes and faced him. "You have a way of cutting through the bullshit that annoys the hell out of me sometimes."

Jake grinned. "It takes talent, sis."

She picked up one of the offending harnesses and made like she was going to throw it at him. "Yeah?"

"Hey, just take your time. Things work themselves out if you go at them slowly. With a little patience."

"Patience has never been my strong suit."

He slid a finger over his tablet and straightened. "I'll have Claire check these numbers later. She's the brain in this one-horse town." He faced her. "So what do you think about working in the shed?"

"I like it. I haven't killed anybody yet, but it's only been just over a week."

"I'm happy with your work, Cass."

Warmth bloomed in her chest. "Thanks, bro."

"You're good with the customers, especially the kids. That takes a certain kind of talent."

"I admit I like working with them. In small doses, they're pretty cool. And when they conquer the kids' course? They look so proud and happy."

"So do you."

She dropped her gaze and worked her fingers in the closest harness. "What do you mean?"

"I've seen you cheering for them when they come back in."

She shrugged. "It seems like an appropriate response."

"It is. So do you think you'll stay here?"

"With the adventure courses?"

Jake nodded. "Among other things."

"I'm still not sure. Bill is coming next week."

"What does that have to do with anything?"

"Maybe he'll grant me a reprieve, Jake. And I can get back to my life."

Jake cursed softly. "You know, I have a damn good life right here. I'm a little insulted when you talk about Cypress like it's an internment camp."

"That's not what I mean."

"Then just what do you mean?"

"I don't know where I belong."

"You belong with family."

She turned her attention on the harnesses again. "I guess so."

She felt him approach but didn't face him.

"Look, sis. I know what it's like to feel like you don't belong. Why the hell do you think I was always running away?"

That brought her head up. "You were running away? From what?"

"From everything. From Bill. From Chapman Financial. Hell, from life. This place…" He gazed out the wide front window of the shed, a small smile on his face. "This place forced me to face what I was running from. I needed to find my place and so do you."

"But what if I fail?"

Jake's eyes went wide. "Then you have your family to pick you up and dust you off."

The bell above the door jingled as another customer entered. Her brother moved to the front to greet them, leaving Cassie to the puzzle of the harnesses.

As she worked her fingers slowly and patiently into the webbed straps, she thought about last Tuesday night with Ty.

197

He'd been an amazing lover, but that was no surprise. The guy had moves and seemed to know just how to touch her. The talk after that first time had been an eye-opener, though. She would never have imagined that he harbored such guilt about his sister's mistakes. And his own, although he was just a kid when he'd gone away to college.

As for her own romps through Europe? She'd been a kid too, but the boarding schools never could hold her interest. Not the studies and not the teachers. Not even the other lonely kids acting out against their own parents' crap. And when she'd gotten old enough to quit going to school altogether? Her father had simply footed the bill as she made her careless way through sparkling cities and glittering night clubs.

It was amazing, but she didn't miss that life. Not at the moment. She was enjoying getting closer to her family and getting to know Ty. As for her gainful employment? That was a matter still up for debate.

She did like working here, though. The people were friendly and the setting was pretty. Relaxing, too. She could hear herself think in the quiet of Cypress Corners. She wasn't always eager to hear just what she was thinking, though. Coming up with reasons to avoid Ty was a big one. Why, she didn't know. Okay, she did. He scared her. He was just so solid and real. It was like he was a whole different breed from the selfish boys she'd known all her life. He was intense, too. Committed, to his work and to his family. He was a lot like her brother Rick that way. She had no doubt in her mind that Rick would die before he let anything bad happen to Harmony or Nick. Ty was like Jake too, though. A little rough around the edges with charm to spare. She'd never been with a guy like him. That was for sure.

"Hey Cassie, can you get these guys set up?" Jake called to her.

She smiled at the two college-age boys checking her out. She wore a camp shirt with khaki shorts and Keds, and her hair was up in a ponytail. They probably thought she was their age, and she wasn't going to correct that assumption. She was going to use it to her advantage, though. Get them to buy a few extras to go with their adventure today. If she'd learned anything from Rick, it was that if there was something a customer really wanted you could get them to buy it.

She flashed them a smile. "Hi, I'm Cassie. How can I help you."

"We want to do one of the adventure courses."

Leading them to the pamphlets outlining the different

adventures, she winked. "What are you up for?"

They stared at her for a beat, and then grinned.

By the time they were equipped and ready to go, she'd signed them up for the obstacle climb, the rope bridge and the course that gave them a 6-mile run. She was tired just imagining doing all of those, but they looked very excited as they turned their attention from her to the challenges ahead.

"Nice job," Jake said, coming alongside her. "Why don't you take off. Grab something for lunch and be back around one?"

"Thank, boss." She smiled. "Bring you a burger?"

"Ah, Cassie. You know the way to your brother's heart."

"Heart attack, maybe. Don't worry. I won't tell Claire."

"Hey, beef is good for making babies."

She laughed. "If you say so. I'll see you at one."

Leaving the shed, she headed back to the golf cart she used to get around the property. It was painted in bursts of color, with palm trees and muddy water depicted all over the sides and hood. It was geared for the adventure courses and was themed for excitement. She liked it and she liked working with Jake. For the time-being, this would suit her. As for the rest of her life?

That remained to be seen.

***

Ty walked into the shed around four and found Jake at the counter. By the way Jake's clothes were smudged with dirt and his hair was messed, he could guess he'd taken a run or two on the courses this afternoon.

"Hey, Jake."

Jake smiled. "Ty. Looking for Cassie?"

Ty just shook his head. He wasn't going to admit to her brother that he had hoped for a glimpse of her today. The work week was drawing to a close and he hadn't had the chance to get her alone since Tuesday night.

"Actually, I'd like a hard workout. I just finished a hellish tour with a couple of dude-bros."

Jake chuckled. "Did they try to jump in one of the lakes?"

"How did you guess? They wanted to wrestle a gator, like I would ever let that happen."

"There must be a fraternity visiting. We just had some college guys in to run the courses."

"I'm sure you gave them the low-down on safety."

"Actually, Cassie handled it."

Jake looked pretty proud of his sister and that made Ty feel good, too.

"How's she working out?"

"I think she might have found her niche. No phone calls to mess up. No sales pitches either, although she's really good at signing people up for more than they came in for. And they're always happy when they're done, too. She has a gift, I think."

"She's pretty amazing."

Jake raised his brows and shot him a look. Ty just shrugged.

"I'm not going to pretend I don't like her, Jake. I couldn't if I tried."

"Yeah, you have that goofy look going on."

Ty grunted at him. "Just set me up?"

"Sure. What do you want today?"

"I think I'll tackle the big climbing structure. I ran 10 miles yesterday and my left ankle is a little tender."

"You should head over to the swim club then."

"I'll be fine to climb."

"Okay." Jake went over to the harnesses and grabbed one made for someone of Ty's build and weight. "Here you go. Grab a helmet. I see the shoes. You have gloves?"

Ty pulled the pair out of the back pocket of his shorts. "Yep."

"Then have at it."

Ty fastened the strap on the helmet and pulled on his gloves. He'd gone to the locker he kept in the fitness center and changed out of his Institute uniform and into gym shorts and a snug T-shirt. He needed to focus and getting up on the wall always did it for him. The run yesterday cleared his head like he'd expected but he still felt a tingle of pent-up energy. It was probably withdrawal after loving Cassie all Tuesday night. He smiled to himself. Yeah, he probably shouldn't share that with her brother, either.

He exited the shed and turned down the path toward the climbing walls. There were several set up on the courses, of differing heights and skill levels. There were spotters and assistants here too, along with belayers, so everyone would be safe.

As he passed the wall for moderate skill levels, he caught sight of a body he was starting to know pretty well. Firm, smooth legs. Round, sweet ass. Yep. Cassie was halfway up on the wall, clinging like a bunch of Spanish moss. She wasn't moving.

Ty looked over the apparatus. Her harness was tied to a top rope threaded to a carabiner at the top of the structure. The other end of the rope was held by a belayer. In this case, the guy was in his early twenties and looked pretty worried. He held on tight to Cassie's rope, which was threaded through the belay device on his harness.

"She okay?" Ty asked him.

"She said she didn't need any instructions." The guy shrugged. "Then she just started climbing."

"And then?"

"And then she froze. She refuses to climb down and won't let anybody go up there to help her."

Ty nodded and walked closer until he was directly under her. She wore climbing shoes, at least. A pair of loaners from the shed. Her camp shirt was a little loose, though. She was stuck almost halfway up the wall, about twelve feet off the ground. From this angle he could see straight up her back. Today's bra was purple.

"Hey there, Cassie," he called up to her.

She jerked, and then let out a little yelp. "H-hey, Ty. What's up?"

He snorted. "You, apparently. Why are you climbing this wall?"

She turned her head, still holding tight to the wall. She was looking down at him now, and he could see her brow was furrowed beneath her helmet.

"It seemed like a good idea at the time."

Placing his hands on his hips, he stepped over to the side so he could look up into her face. "And now?"

"N-now?" She made that yelping sound again as she tried to move her left foot. "Now, not so much."

Ty put on his harness and threaded one of the top ropes through. He waved over another belayer and handed him the other end. "I'm going up to get her. Hold onto this for me."

The other belayer nodded and secured the rope into his harness. Ty started to climb, coming up to Cassie's level in just a few steps. He stopped right next to her.

"Hey, there," he said, making sure to show her how relaxed he was in his harness. "You okay?"

She gave a quick shake of her head, like she was afraid to move. "Get. Me. Down."

He smiled. "You got it. You have to trust me, though."

Her eyes met his and the jolt nearly sent him falling to the ground. "I trust you, Ty."

Swallowing, he focused on maneuvering so that he was over her. He cradled her with his body and felt her relax a fraction against him.

"We're going to climb down," he said, for her benefit and for the two belayers on the ground.

The guys called up to them that they were ready and he placed his right hand over Cassie's.

"You need to let go."

"I can't," she squeaked.

"You can. I've got you."

She gave a shaky nod, which was something at least. "O-okay."

With his hand on hers, he put his weight to the left and smoothly moved their right hands down to another hold.

"That feels better," she said, easing a bit more.

"Your arms must have felt pretty stretched."

"Like they were going to pop out of their sockets."

"We can't have that," he said, his mouth close to the back of her neck. He could smell her and almost taste the dewy sweat he saw there. "Now the left."

He repeated the move with their left sides, easing the pressure on that arm, too. The feet were going to be trickier but he calmly told her what to do and she began to anticipate his every move as they slowly made their way down the wall.

He managed to crab-walk her down the wall, one hold at a

time, until they were only a foot above the ground. Nodding to his belayer he jumped down, wincing as his ankle gave a little protest. He placed his hands on Cassie's waist. Her belayer lessened the tension and Ty was able to pull her down to solid ground.

"There." He began to untie her harness. "You did it."

"I did it," she said, her voice holding a touch of awe. "You did it. I'd still be stuck up there like a bug on a windshield if you hadn't come along."

Ty handed the rope to the belayer, who looked so relieved he might faint. "They would have called Jake and he would have come up for you."

She nodded, her eyes shiny. "I know. There are people who would actually come to my rescue. Like you."

Ty wanted to kiss her right then. Instead he stepped back and unfastened his own harness. "Thanks," he said to his belayer as he handed him the rope. "Good work."

Both of the other guys exchanged looks of relief as they checked over the gear. Ty helped Cassie out of the harness, laughing when she reached behind to adjust her shorts.

"Jeez, talk about a wedgie. No wonder the harnesses get all tangled." He laughed as she unclipped the chin strap of her helmet. "Remind me to do that again. Real soon."

"If you'd started on one of the beginner walls, maybe you wouldn't have gotten stuck."

"Not stuck, Ty. Scared."

"Okay, scared. It's nothing to be ashamed of. Everybody needs a little help now and then."

She placed a hand in the middle of his chest, leaning into him. "I'm glad you were here to help me today."

Suddenly he didn't care who was watching. He leaned down and kissed her. She was sweet and hot and she let out that little purr sound she sometimes made when she was excited.

Pulling back, he found her grinning up at him.

"What?"

"You look hot in that helmet, Ty."

He placed his hand on top of his head and laughed. Their audience wasn't the only thing he'd forgotten. "A real fashion statement."

She smiled, and then nodded to the belayers. "Thanks, guys."

"Sure."

"Yeah, any time."

They both couldn't look right at her and Ty could guess the

reason. Her camp shirt was plastered to the front of her from sweat and that pretty purple bra was on display.

"Let me walk you back to the shed. You're still a little shaky."

She stopped him with a hand on his arm. "You're limping."

He shrugged. "I tweaked my ankle yesterday on my run. It's nothing."

"Your ankle was injured and you still helped me?"

"I didn't give it a passing thought."

She gave a sweet little gasp, and then let his arm go as they walked on.

"Jake is going to kill me," she said in a low voice as they stepped into the shed.

"He's not going to kill you."

"Why am I not going to kill her?" Jake asked, frowning.

"Nothing major," Ty said. "Cassie was up on one of the walls and she got a little nervous."

"I was scared out of my mind," Cassie said with a smile that told him she was slowly getting over it. "Ty came to my rescue."

"Yeah?" Jake came around the counter and clapped Ty on the shoulder. "Thanks, man. I owe you."

"It was nothing," Ty answered.

Cassie clicked her tongue. "Okay, if you're both done being all testosteron-y, I'll put our gear away and help close down."

"Weren't you going for a climb, Ty?"

"You should have told him not to climb, Jake. His ankle is sore."

"I'm fine, Cassie," Ty told her. "But I've had all the excitement I can handle for today, thanks."

Cassie stared at him. Hard. "I hope that's not true."

Ty kept his expression even as her brother watched him over her shoulder. "Maybe you want to do dinner later? At the tavern?"

"Sure." She leaned closer, ignoring her brother who now made a show of straightening the counter and looking anywhere but at his little sister and Ty. "But how about pizza out by the far lakeshore?"

Ty couldn't keep the grin off his face. "Sounds good."

She kissed him again, just a quick peck, and went over to the equipment wall. When Ty dragged his eyes off of her he found Jake with his arms crossed, one brow arched.

"See you, Jake."

"Yeah, yeah," Jake answered.

Still grinning, Ty left the shed and headed back to the fitness center. His ankle gave a twinge but he ignored it. If this afternoon's rescue mission didn't prove it to him, nothing would.

Cassie Chapman knocked him off his feet.

Chapter 15

They picked up a pizza and ate it out on the back porch of the tent-cabin. The sun was just beginning to dip into the lake as Cassie stretched out in one of the two Adirondack chairs.

"This is just lovely, Ty." She took in a deep breath and let out all the stress she'd been feeling since dangling above the sandy ground of the courses. "This was a great idea."

"It was yours, but I have to agree."

She laughed and took another slice of pizza. "What are you up to this weekend? Do you have Riley tomorrow?"

"Her father called Thursday night. He told my mother that we could have her from ten o'clock until five."

"That's not very long."

"It's longer than he usually gives us with her."

She could feel the pain and frustration coming off of him. "It's none of my business, but I have to say that just sucks."

"Yeah, it does. There's nothing I can do about it, though."

"What about visitation rights? Don't you have any?"

Ty shook his head, the expression on his face showing how sad the situation made him. "Not at all."

"So Riley's father has full custody?"

Ty lifted his beer bottle to his lips and took a long sip.

"There's no such thing as child custody in Florida."

"What? Why the hell not?"

He raised his brows. "There just isn't. My mother doesn't even have rights."

"But she's Riley's grandmother! That doesn't make any sense."

"There are grandparents' rights laws on the books but they're unconstitutional. It's a shitty system but one we have no choice but to honor."

"And if you approached Riley's father and demanded visitation?"

Ty laughed but there didn't seem to be any humor in it. "You don't know this guy. If I demand anything from Hank he'll fix it so we never see Riley again."

She scowled. "This guy sounds like a prick."

"He is. But he's a good ol' boy with lots of connections in town. His family practically founded St. Cloud. He can drink and have parties out at his place where the cops get called but nothing sticks. We're at his mercy."

Cassie drank more of her beer, and then set the bottle down on the deck. "You know, our father had nothing to do with us aside from paying bills. He's a prick, too. Maybe my brothers

213

and I were better off."

"Better off ignored by your father?"

She snorted. "Ignored? Yeah, pretty much. Bill had lots of money to throw at us, though. All the toys we could ever want. The fanciest schools. Pricey tutors. You name it."

"Sounds like something out of a movie."

"I guess it was. There was no love there, though. Not from him. Our mother more than made up for his lack of affection, though. Maybe a little bit too much sometimes."

"How do you mean?"

Cassie felt a little guilty talking about her poor, put-upon mother but sitting here with Ty felt like a very safe place. She wouldn't try to figure out why just now, though. She'd just take advantage of his easygoing nature and spill her guts.

"Our mother was very attached to all of us. It could get a little stifling at times. Rick bore the brunt of it, I suppose. Guilt-tripped into working for Bill right out of college like an indentured servant."

"He did well with Chapman, though. Didn't he?"

"He made lots of money. For himself and our dad and the investors. But he was miserable. Even from far away, I could sense that anytime we connected."

Ty looked thoughtful for a second. "He's happy now."

"Yeah, because he got away from Bill and all that bullshit. Jake did too, although his own brand of rebellion almost got him killed a couple of times."

"I'd heard about that, too." Ty smiled a little. "Your brothers don't do anything by half-measure, do they?"

"None of us do." She wiped her hands and leaned back in the chair. "I did some crazy stupid things to get away from Bill. And to get his attention. How pathetic is that?"

Ty reached over to cover her hand with his. "You're not pathetic. You've made some mistakes but you're not that scared little girl anymore."

She looked at him sharply. "Who said I was scared?"

He shrugged. "Weren't you? I would be, so far away from my family."

"I guess so. You see so much more than I want to show."

"There's nothing you can show me that would send me running, Cassie."

He looked so earnest right then. The sunset picked up the streaks in his hair and the stubble on his cheeks. His eyes were intense and his beautiful mouth was serious.

"Thanks," she said for lack of anything more clever.

They were quiet for a few long minutes, just drinking their beer and staring out over the lake. It was really quite pretty out here. Wild yet inviting. It was unlike any place she'd ever been before.

"So when did you lose your mother?" he finally asked.

"About three years after Bill left us for good. I was nine years old."

"That's pretty young. Who took care of you?"

She found a smile. "Rick, mostly. He was always so much more serious than me and Jake, but he seemed to grow up really fast. Our father was technically handed custody but he didn't spend any real time with us. Nannies and tutors raised us, so to speak."

"That sucks, but you and your brothers are close."

That warmth filled her chest as it had when she sat with her brothers outside the coffee shop the other day. "We are. Now. Jake and I are a lot alike but he and Rick were closest, I think. I was too busy burning my way through Europe to bother with holidays and stuff."

"Then you'll have to stay through the holidays here in Cypress."

"That's almost seven months from now."

He got a little worry line between his brows. "You won't be here?"

"I honestly don't know." Her eyes pricked and she looked back out at the lake. "I don't know where I'll be."

Ty grew really quiet. Even more than usual. Chancing a look at him, she thought he almost looked sad. Would he miss her if she left? No one ever missed her.

"You okay?" she asked.

He faced her with that grin made her stomach flip, a dimple peeping at her in one cheek. "I'm better than okay. I'm eating pizza and drinking beer out by the lake with the prettiest girl I've ever seen."

"You're my hero, you know."

He gave a slow nod. "I know. Saved you from yourself."

"Myself?" She hit him on the arm. "I didn't know how tough that wall was."

"And you work in the shed?"

She had to allow that one. "Yeah, I know. I'm sure Jake will read me the riot act but good on Monday morning."

"Then you're off this weekend?"

"Yep."

"Then come to Old Town Village with me and Riley

tomorrow."

"What's that?"

"It's this quirky place over in Kissimmee. It has rides and games and old-fashioned shops. I know, it sounds lame but it's pretty fun."

"Wait. They have car shows too, right?"

"Some weekends. I don't think they have one tomorrow, though."

Cassie nodded. "Claire and Jake take her father there sometimes. I heard them talking about it."

"I think they do. What do you say?"

"A whole day with Riley, sure. She's adorable. But you?" she teased. "I don't know. You're kind of a stick in the mud. All about safety and nature. A real know-it-all."

"Oh, yeah?"

"Yeah. I'll definitely have to think about it."

He growled and reached over, pulling her onto his lap. "I can remind you of how much fun I can be." He buried his face in the crook of her neck and she let out a little giggle. "I can show you just how much I know, too."

A flash of heat seemed to bubble up between them and it wasn't from the burst of orange and pink from the setting sun.

She framed his face with her hands, and then drove her fingers into his hair. "Show me."

***

Ty was whistling as he poured himself a coffee in his mother's kitchen. Last night with Cassie had been a revelation, and not just the sex. She'd opened up to him about her childhood, which sounded pretty fucked-up to him. He'd had two wonderful parents and still enjoyed being with his mother. The huge fly in the ointment was the shit Tracy put them through, before and after her death. Even thoughts about Tracy and his own guilt about how she'd turned out couldn't dim his smile this morning.

"I expected you to stay out at your love shack last night," his mother said as she came down the stairs.

He managed to keep his smile as he shook his head at her. "It's Saturday, Mom. We have Riley today and I have to pick her up for ten."

"Yes, I know. Will you see Cassie today, too?"

He blinked at her. "Can you read minds now?"

She laughed, settling on one of the stools at the tall counter. "I don't have to. The two of you are dating. Everybody knows that now."

"I'm not going to argue with everybody, then. We're taking Riley to Old Town Village."

Her face lit up. "Oh, she'll love that!"

"I know it's a lot of walking, but do you want to come with us?"

She shook her head. "No, dear. You three go have fun. Just promise to bring our little angel here before you go back to Hank's? I know it's out of the way."

Ty put down his mug. "Count on it. Besides, we have her until five and the kid will probably poop out not long after lunch."

His mother's face was bright. "Good. Then maybe after you drop her off you and Cassie can have a proper date."

"A proper date? I've taken her out to dinner, you know. The Boathouse."

"I know." She winked. "Everybody knows."

Ty finished his coffee and put his mug in the sink. "I'm going to go pick up Cassie and then we're heading out."

"Put sunblock on Riley, Ty. And maybe take that little hat I bought her."

"Why don't you go grab some stuff for her and I'll bring them along."

He rarely saw his mother move as fast as she did to gather some things for Riley. In just a couple of minutes Ty was holding onto a hot pink tote bag covered with white polka dots and Minnie Mouse faces.

Slinging it over his shoulder, he let out a groan. "The things I do for my niece."

His mother pushed at his shoulder. "Go. Have fun."

"I'm taking your car, so just call or text me if you need anything."

"I'll be fine, Ty. I'll just sit out on the porch, I think. It's a lovely day."

"Good. I'll call when we're on our way home."

"Home." The light in his mother's eyes dimmed a little. "I wish this was her home."

"She's safe and well taken care of at Hank's, Mom. That's what we have to focus on."

She sniffed, and then nodded. "You're right. You're always right."

He shook his head. "Always right, huh? I'll remember that the next time you disagree with me about something."

"Never mind. Now, shoo."

He pulled his mother's Camry out of the garage, and then hit the windows and breathed in. The air was fresh this morning, although it would probably get pretty warm come the afternoon. That was spring in Central Florida. As he approached Rick and Harmony's, he saw Cassie waiting for him on the porch. She stood when he stopped the car and he took a few seconds to just look at her.

All that wavy dark hair was pulled up off her face in a ponytail and she wore a purple T-shirt and denim shorts. The shirt was worn and had French words scrawled across it. It might be the same one she'd been wearing when he'd picked her up at the airport, but he couldn't be sure. There had been so much else to notice about her that afternoon. Damn, her legs looked long with those shorts and little sneakers.

Before he could get out of the car she was running toward him. She got in and fastened her seatbelt, a grin on her face.

"Hey, there!" She leaned in and kissed him right on the mouth. "Isn't it a nice morning?"

"It is. Thanks for coming."

"This is going to be fun, Ty. Rick and Harmony gave me the lowdown on the best rides."

"Yeah well, promise me you won't try the zip line."

She waved a hand. "No worries there. I think I've had

222

enough with ropes and heights to last a lifetime."

He pulled away from the curb and turned the car around to head out to St. Cloud. She picked up the straps to the pink tote and let out a short laugh.

"This yours?" she asked. "I wouldn't have thought pink was your signature color."

"Ha. No, it's Riley's. Please say you'll carry it around today?"

She nodded. "Sure thing. I love Minnie. She's a classic."

"Thanks. I hope you're up for carnival food."

"What, like candy apples and popcorn and stuff?"

"Mostly. There are a few restaurants too. And a couple of bars, believe it or not."

"Anything is fine with me. I'm determined to go with the flow today."

"Just today?"

"Are you saying I'm a tight ass?"

He threw her a grin. "Not touching that one, sweetheart."

She chuckled. "So how far is Riley's dad's place?"

"Not too. About ten minutes from Cypress."

"So close?" She clicked her tongue. "And you still only get to see her a little bit?"

"Yeah."

He didn't notice how tightly he was gripping the steering wheel until he felt Cassie's fingers on his knuckles.

"Easy there." She leaned back in her seat. "Will I get to meet this Hank person?"

"Probably, so I'll apologize in advance."

"For what?"

"He's kind of a pig."

"Yikes."

"Considers himself a lady's man. He's much older than my sister was. Probably late forties, I'd guess."

"He sounds lovely."

"I try not to interact with him much. His wife is a quiet thing. I doubt she'll come out to meet you."

"He's married?"

"Yep. Has been for decades."

"He just gets better and better."

Ty smiled a little. She was good for him, especially today. Seeing the situation with fresh eyes and giving her opinion openly could only be a good thing. As long as she didn't give her opinion to Hank.

"We'll make it quick. Hank is never one to stick around

once I pick Riley up."

"Where does he go?"

"Damned if I know. Today I think he's going to another gun show up in Orlando. The guy loves his firearms."

Cassie clicked her tongue again. "We'll have to make sure Riley has a great time with her Uncle Ty."

"Yep. We will."

When he pulled the car up the long drive to Hank's place, Riley was already waiting on the porch. There was no sign of Hank.

Stopping the car, he stepped out. "Hey, sweetie. Where's your dad?"

"Had to go up to Orlando. Mommy Linda is inside, though."

He walked toward the porch as he heard Cassie open her door. Riley's face lit up when she saw Cassie.

"Cassie!" She flew down the porch steps and wrapped herself around Cassie's waist. "I didn't know you were coming!"

Cassie stroked her hand over Riley's hair. "Your Uncle Ty made Old Town Village sound so great, how could I refuse his invitation?"

The screen door creaked as Linda came out onto the porch.

"Good morning, Linda," Ty said.

The woman looked tired but she nodded. "Hello."

"Linda, this is Cassie Chapman. A friend of mine. Cassie, this is Linda Busey."

"Nice to meet you," Cassie said.

Linda nodded. "You guys have fun today. Be good, Riley. Okay?"

"Yes, Mommy Linda."

Riley released Cassie. She scrambled up onto the porch and hugged Linda. After a beat, Linda patted her little shoulders.

"Go on. We'll see you at five, right Ty?"

He could see by the determination in her gaze that she wasn't going to fudge on the return time. No, Hank had laid down the law and she was going to uphold it.

"Five it is, Linda."

She looked relieved when Riley came back down to him and Cassie. Ty took the little girl's hand and led her over to the car. Buckling her into her car seat, he took a second to give her a couple of loud kisses that made her giggle.

"All set?" he asked her.

Riley nodded and he got back behind the wheel. He could see the questions in Cassie's mind as they drove away from Hank's house. He also knew with certainty that she wouldn't bring them up within Riley's hearing. He didn't really know how he knew so much about Cassie's character but he just did. She was an open book, to him at least.

"All set, Cassie?"

She smiled at him. "Yep. Let's go have some fun."

Sending her a look of gratitude, he focused on the ride into Kissimmee. There would be enough time to talk about the mess that was just on display on Hank's porch. For now, he would enjoy a day with his two favorite girls in the world. He didn't know when Hank would give them a chance to actually go somewhere again. And as for Cassie? After her comment about not being here for the holidays, he didn't even know how long he had with her.

He would just enjoy the present and leave the worries for later.

Chapter 16

Cassie listened while Riley chattered about something from the backseat, her mind working around the situation she'd just witnessed. It was clear that Riley was safe and clean and taken care of but she didn't see a whole lot of love coming from Hank's wife. No, Mommy Linda thought of Riley as an obligation and nothing more.

"Hey, sweetie," Cassie said, leaning over to smile at the little girl. "I hear you're up for some rides."

"The merry-go-round for sure," she said. "Can we ride it three times, Uncle Ty?"

"You might get a little dizzy, honey. We'll see how it goes."

"Sure," Riley said.

Cassie turned forward again, sliding a glance at Ty. "You're a good uncle."

"It's easy." He glanced into the backseat, and then faced forward. "As long as she doesn't eat too much cotton candy."

He'd said it loud enough for Riley to hear and she giggled. "Oh, Uncle Ty! You know I only eat it because it's pink. I love pink."

"What about the blue kind?" Cassie asked her. "That's pretty tasty, too."

"We'll have to have the blue kind too!" Riley said.

"Great," Ty grumbled with a sideways smile.

The ride to Old Town Village wasn't too long, and about fifteen minutes after picking up Riley they came upon the huge Ferris wheel set nearly on the street.

"We're here, we're here!" Riley piped up from the backseat.

"Apparently," Cassie said.

Ty pulled into the lot, which already had a lot of cars parked in its spaces. He shut off the engine and turned to smile at Riley.

"Ready for some fun?"

Cassie watched as the little girl practically vibrated with excitement. While Ty got Riley out of her seat Cassie shouldered the pink Minnie bag.

"Wait," Ty said. "Sunblock."

Cassie withdrew the bottle she found at the bottom of the bag and slathered it on Riley's arms, legs and face. The pink bucket hat in the bag looked adorable perched on top of her blond waves.

"Ready, pretty girl?" Cassie asked.

Riley beamed at her, reaching out a hand to grab onto hers. Cassie looked at Ty, who nodded. Ty took Riley's other hand in his, and the three of them started for the entrance of the place.

Riley skipped along between them and Cassie was seized with a completely foreign kind of yearning. She had to be going crazy if she thought she was looking for this kind of life. It was nothing like she'd ever wanted. The right guy, a sweet kid who looked like him. Feeling like she was as much the center of their universe as the man and child were to her.

"Over there, Cassie!" Riley said, tugging on her arm.

"Hmm?" She looked up to find the little girl and Ty both looking at her with matching looks of confusion. "Where are we going?"

"The merry-go-round, Cassie," Riley said in her best put-upon voice. "We have to go before I have something to eat."

Cassie arched a brow. "Oh, yeah? Trouble a-brewing?"

"Not if we're careful," Ty put in with a crooked smile.

The carousel was an old-fashioned beauty with painted horses and done up with sculpted flowers and ribbons.

"This is so pretty, Riley! No wonder you wanted to ride this first."

Riley nodded, wiggling and hopping from foot to foot while Ty bought them all tickets. Ty put the little girl up on the horse she chose, pink of course, and stood beside her.

"Mount up, Cassie," he said.

She laughed and swung her leg over the horse on the other side of Riley's mount. With a slight jerk, the carousel started and the sounds of calliope music filled the air. Around and around they went, and Cassie couldn't help but add her laughter to Riley's as the ride came to its inevitable stop.

"You rode so good, Cassie," Riley said, her eyes big.

"And you're a top-notch horsewoman yourself."

Cassie scooped the little girl into her arms and swung her down to solid ground. "Where to next?"

Ty stepped down and took Cassie's hand this time as she held Riley's. It was nice, holding hands with a guy.

"I'm thinking the Ferris wheel," Ty said.

"No way, man," Cassie said. "Nuh-uh."

"Please, please, please!" Riley said.

Cassie gave a shudder. "I'm not good with heights, sweetie. Just ask your Uncle Ty."

Ty smirked at her, and then looked down at Riley. "Cassie was stuck up on one of the climbing walls yesterday. I think she thought she was a mountain goat."

Riley giggled and Cassie put a hand on her hip. "I just don't think I want to go up there."

Riley looked up at her with a serious expression. "It'll be

okay, Cassie. Uncle Ty would never let anything happen to you or me."

"That's true," Ty said.

Cassie could only nod. She'd never seen such trust in her life. And to be included under Ty's protection? That made her feel all kinds of things she shouldn't.

"If you promise," she told the little girl, "Then, okay."

All three of them survived the ride, to Cassie's relief. By the time their bucket finished its second rotation, they were stepping down from the rocking thing.

"You did it!" Riley hugged Cassie's legs and she nearly fell over. "I knew Uncle Ty would keep you safe."

The little girl's words made her feel like she was still up on the wheel. Oh, she wanted to grab on to Ty and let him fix everything for her. He was the perfect son and uncle. The perfect friend. The perfect lover. He was almost too good to be true. And speaking of true, she had to face one huge fact.

He was way too good for her.

***

After lunch at the burger place set just off the midway of the kiddy rides, Riley looked like she was beginning to wear out. Cassie was a little quiet too, but she'd been subdued since they

got off the Ferris wheel. Maybe she was afraid of heights after
all. He'd have to make sure she held on tight to him tonight,
then. He planned on sending her to the ceiling.

After a round on the hopping ladybug ride, Ty figured it was
time to go back to Cypress.

"Let's head on over to Grandma's, sweetie," he said to
Riley, steering her toward the parking lot.

Riley started to argue but when she yawned Ty knew he had
her. She climbed into the backseat and settled into her car seat
without a peep. Cassie cracked open one of the bottles of water
she'd had the forethought to buy and handed it to Riley.

"Drink, honey," she said. "I know I get tired when I'm
dehydrated."

Riley drank, and handed her back the bottle. "I'm wet now."

Cassie chuckled. Ty guessed they both knew Riley didn't
mean she wet her pants. In fact, Cassie had taken her to the
ladies' room just before the bug ride.

"Grandma probably made cookies today," Ty said.

"Chocolate chip?" Riley asked around another yawn.

"Yeah. And you can take some back home with you."

"I want to sleep at your house, Uncle Ty."

Ty bit back the words he wanted to say about her selfish

233

father but instead he took a calming breath. He was really glad the little girl couldn't see his expression at that angle.

"Another time, sweetie," he said. "I promise."

Cassie touched his hand like she had earlier and he felt better. That was weird, that she could affect him like that. With just a look or a touch she made him feel better. Maybe it was because he could share his frustrations with her about Riley and the visitation situation. Lord knew he couldn't share them with his mother.

His mother worried enough about the little girl to also worry about Ty's feelings. He agreed with her when she voiced her disappointment, and when she glossed over her own sadness when he brought Riley back home he did likewise. It was nice to have someone who didn't judge him and even got a little pissed off on his behalf.

The car ride back to St. Cloud was nothing like the one out to Kissimmee this morning. Riley was nodding off in the back and Cassie was quiet, too.

"Do you want to get dinner after I take Riley home?" he asked.

Cassie looked over and shrugged. "Sure. Where?"

"How about the End Zone? It's a sports bar in St. Cloud. We

can shoot a couple games of pool."

"You shoot pool?"

"A little. You?"

She smiled. "Actually, it's called billiards in the UK. Peasant."

He laughed. "Okay, well we'll play American pool and I'll give you some pointers."

"I can handle my balls, Ty. Can you?"

He shook his head. "Not touching that one, either."

They shared a smile and he glanced in the rearview mirror again. Riley was staring out the window but it was clear from her gaze that she was starting to zone out. This had been a really great day, for his niece and for him. He loved to spend time with Riley but when he added Cassie to the mix? Today was just about as perfect as it could get. He thought about Cassie's teasing and looked forward to tonight and making the day even more perfect.

After his mother fussed over Riley and Cassie both, they took the little girl back to Hank's. On the short ride to the End Zone, Ty bit back the usual pain and frustration he felt whenever he dropped Riley off at her father's.

"Talk to me, Ty," Cassie said.

"It tears me up, Cassie. Every time I drop her off at Hank's I want to either cry or punch something."

"You know, you can do either one of those with me. I won't judge."

He slid her a look. Her face was open and her expression clear. It was the picture of support. Support he'd never had because he'd always had to be the strong one for his mother.

"Thanks, but I think I'm okay now."

Cassie nodded. "Your mother adores that little girl. You do, too."

"Yeah, and we have to beg Hank for every scrap of time with her."

"Maybe you should sit down and talk with him."

"With Hank?" Ty scoffed. "If you think that could work, you don't know Hank."

"I don't. I do know he's her father and you have no legalities to stand on. You have no choice."

He shook his head. "Maybe, but I can't talk to Hank. We can't stand each other."

"How long was he with your sister?"

"I have no idea. It wasn't until Tracy died that Hank had anything to do with Riley. He took her, legally, and that's where

236

we are now. Can we drop this?"

"Sure."

Her agreement was laced with something else but he wasn't going to rehash the crap that was the situation with Riley and Hank.

They pulled into the parking lot and Ty saw the usual collection of vehicles filling the spaces. Trucks and motorcycles and SUVs, typical for the laidback city. He shut the car off and left the keys dangling in the ignition.

"I'm sorry, Cassie."

"You don't have to apologize, Ty."

"It's just a sensitive subject for me."

"And I'm an outsider. I get it."

He stared at her. "You're not an outsider."

She blinked rapidly, and then nodded. "I am, but that's okay. I'm used to it."

"If you say so. I see something different, though."

"What, Ty? What do you see?"

"You're connecting with your family." He shot her a grin. "And we're growing close too, or so I thought."

She touched his face, sliding her fingers into his hair the way he liked. "We are. But this conversation is a little deep for a

Saturday night, don't you think?"

He took his cue from her and pulled back. He grabbed the keys and gave her a quick kiss. "Then how about I whoop your pretty little ass in pool?"

She laughed. "Don't count your chickens, or whatever. I have skills you haven't seen."

"Then you may just kill me yet."

Back on steady footing, the two of them went into the sports bar. The End Zone was as dim as usual inside but the large dining room to the right was lined all around with TVs set high on the walls. The screens showed fishing programs and Ultimate Fighting matches along with just about every other sport ever televised. The scent of French fries and buffalo wings hung in the air, along with the ever-present malty beer smell. There weren't many families seated at a few of the wooden tables and booths, but it was a Saturday night. Mostly couples and groups of friends, it looked like.

The long bar stretched along the back wall and the wait staff buzzed around with round trays of food and drink. A couple of the servers nodded a greeting to him and he returned the gesture. Country pop songs were playing on the digital juke box and the crack of ball against ball could be heard through the wide opening to the pool room to the left.

"The End Zone." He put his hand on the small of Cassie's back as he steered her toward an empty table. "Let's grab a table."

"Look who's here!" Claire Chapman called.

Ty looked over to see Jake and his wife sitting at a booth to the right. Cassie's face lit up and she hurried over to them. She might think she was an outsider but nobody seeing how she greeted Jake and Claire, and how they happily greeted her back, would believe it.

"Hi!" Cassie hugged Claire and punched her brother in the arm. "I didn't know you guys were coming here tonight."

"Jake needed a challenge," Claire quipped. "Maybe tonight he can win a game."

Jake rolled his eyes. "Damn, woman. You'll have Ty thinking I can't handle a stick." He got up and sat next to Claire, waving a hand to the now-empty seat across from them. "Let me tell you, Claire is a shark."

"I'm not a shark. Jeez, what will Cassie think of me if you tell them that?"

Cassie slid into the booth and Ty followed. It was a little close and it felt just right.

239

"A shark, huh? Hmm. I played over in England but Ty tells me this isn't snooker."

"Snooker?" Jake chuckled. "Are we having tea and crumpets later?"

"Hardly," Ty said. "Wings and nachos, maybe."

Cassie smiled at him, her eyes sparkling. "Oh, maybe Claire and I will team up and kick both your sorry asses."

Jake groaned. "Man, another one."

Claire reached across and took Cassie's hand in hers. "We Chapman girls have to stick together."

If he hadn't been watching, he would have missed the way Cassie's shoulders tightened just a little bit. Her smile looked warm, though. The girl was afraid to give herself to these people who obviously loved her. It was her own brand of crap and she needed to work through it herself.

He just hoped that she wasn't afraid to give herself to him, too.

Chapter 17

Cassie nibbled on a hot wing, letting the heat from the sauce and the cool bite of blue cheese fill her senses. There was a little pile of skinny bones in front of her and no one was more surprised than she was. She rarely ate this kind of food, simple pub stuff, and it was pretty good. This place was a modern honkytonk, and it was like no other place she'd ever been. Not quite a dive, but it definitely had a dive vibe, if that was a thing. She found she liked it.

"How was Old Town Village?" Claire asked, setting her own plate aside.

"It was a lot of fun." Cassie didn't even skip a beat. She wasn't at all surprised that her family knew what they'd been up to today. Her brothers and their wives talked every day. "Watching Riley enjoying herself was a blast."

"She is a sweet little thing," Claire said. "When can you bring her by again, Ty?"

Ty stiffened beside Cassie, but gave Claire his usual carefree expression. "I'm not sure. Soon, I hope."

Jake sighed dramatically. "Good. She can keep Nick on his toes. That boy wears me out."

"You say that but more than once I found the two of you

241

asleep on Harmony's couch," Claire said.

Jake shrugged and turned a serious expression on his wife. "Chapman men work hard, Claire. We play hard, too."

Claire laughed and waved a hand at him. "Yeah, yeah. So what else did you do at Old Town Village?"

"This and that," Cassie answered. "The merry-go-round and those little cars that look like ladybugs."

"Cassie went up in the Ferris wheel," Ty put in.

Jake's brows rose. "Yeah? After yesterday's climb? Good for you, sis. Back on the horse."

Cassie licked the sauce off her fingers and wiped her hands. "I didn't climb the wheel, Jake. I just sat there and let the machine do the work."

Jake laughed. "Next time you want to climb let me get you on the beginner's wall, okay?"

"I won't be climbing again." She nudged Ty with her shoulder. "Even if big, strong nature boy here comes to my rescue again."

"You are her hero, Ty," Claire said. "Now let's see if you two tough guys can beat two delicate flowers at a real challenge. What do you say, Cassie?"

Cassie grinned and took the last sip of her beer. "Bring it."

The pool room was pretty much what she'd expected. Six tables were lined up down the middle of the big room, with wide shaded lights hanging low above each one. It was noisy with chatter and laughter and the crack of billiard balls. Several games were going on, and there were about eight guys and half as many girls scattered around five of the tables. The closest one was just opening up as they entered, and Ty said hello and thanks to the guys vacating the table.

"Oh, good!" Claire grabbed two cues from the wall and handed one to Cassie. "Here. Rack those balls, boys."

Jake snickered. "That's what she said."

Cassie clicked her tongue at her brother and leaned on her cue stick, eyeing the table. "I think I know how to play eight ball."

"Then we'll play eight ball," Ty said.

She watched him as he racked the balls. He looked a little more relaxed now. She was glad. His nerves had been stretched taut ever since they'd dropped Riley back at her father's. Her putting her nose in his business hadn't helped matters, either.

Claire took the first shot and sank one of the striped balls. Purple and white, the twelve ball.

"We're stripes, Cassie," she grinned.

Jake shook his head. "Just sit tight and watch them, Ty. Claire doesn't give the table up easily."

Claire winked at her husband, and then proceeded to sink the ten and eleven balls too. Then Jake came close and whispered something in her ear that made her blush and scratch on the shot. The cue ball popped into the side pocket and Claire stomped one foot.

"Damn you, Jake Chapman."

Claire didn't look angry, though. In fact, the heat in her eyes showed that whatever Jake had whispered wasn't about their pool game.

"You take the shot, Ty," Jake said. "Let's see what you've got."

Cassie watched Ty as he leaned over the table to line up his shot. His butt looked mighty fine in his cargo shorts, the fabric stretched just right. His shirt rode up a little bit, too. She wanted to slide her hands up his back and feel his smooth muscles. Test his strength as he flexed and shot.

He sank the number two ball and Cassie groaned. Glancing over his shoulder at her, Ty winked.

"Five ball, right corner," he said, and then sank the ball he'd indicated.

"Now who's the shark?" Cassie grumbled.

Ty chuckled and lined up another shot. Taking a page from her brother's book, Cassie came up really close to him. She put her face right in the crook of his neck, breathed in and sighed.

"Cassie," he said, a warning in his voice.

"You handle that stick mighty fine, Ty," she whispered. "Get it in the pocket every time."

He coughed then and missed his shot. He still smiled, though. "You play hard, Cassie Chapman."

Grinning, she grabbed her cue and wriggled her butt at him. "Watch me."

She and Claire cleaned the table between them but the next game was taken by the guys. By the start of the third game Ty looked relaxed and like he was having a good time. His dimples kept peeping out at her and his hazel eyes sparkled like the stars over the far lakeshore.

"What are you guys up to tomorrow?" Ty asked, directing his question toward her.

"Harmony and Rick are barbecuing," Jake answered. "Why don't you come by?"

"I'd love to."

"Bring your mom, Ty," Claire said. "She's a hoot."

Ty snorted. "Yeah. A real Lettie in training."

"I think she's sweet," Cassie told him. "She loves you and Riley so much."

Ty smiled. "If only we—" He looked out into the bar area, a dark look on his face. "Shit."

Cassie followed his gaze and saw it landed on a burly guy in his forties standing just inside the bar area. He had a buzz cut and a beer belly and, by the way he was holding court with a bunch of other rednecks and the expression on Ty's face, she guessed he could only be Hank Busey.

Riley's father.

***

Ty watched Hank reveling in his element, laughing and boasting and being his usual, blowhard self. Cassie stepped close to him and placed her hand on his arm.

"Why don't you go talk to him?" she asked, keeping her voice low.

He could think of a hundred reasons why not, but none of them made any real sense. He had to talk with Hank and at least the guy looked to be in a good mood. Handing Cassie his cue stick, he made his way toward the bar.

"I will."

He left his friends and made his way toward Hank. "Hey, Hank."

Hank turned with a jerk, his eyes going wide for a second before he wore a shit-eating grin. "Walsh. Haven't seen you here in a while."

"I'm here with friends."

Hank looked past him into the pool room, and then faced Ty again with a sly expression. "Friends, huh? I've been watching that hottie you're playing with. She looks familiar. Now, where have I seen her before? Hmm."

Ty took in a calming breath. "Can we talk for a few minutes?"

Hank drained his beer and set his bottle back on the bar. "Sure thing. Buy me another beer and we'll go have a chat."

Ty dug out his wallet and paid for Hank's beer. "Two more, please."

The girl handed him two bottles and Ty brought them over to where Hank was now seated at one of the booths. He handed Hank one bottle, which Hank cracked open. As he took a long drink, Ty sat down across from him and set the other bottle on the table.

"I want to talk about Riley, Hank."

"What about her?"

"We want to see her more often than once a week. And for longer than just a few hours at a time."

"Look, Tracy didn't say anything to me about the kid when she was alive. You and your family had her all to yourselves until your sister kissed that phone pole. Now she lives with me."

Ty bit back a sharp response to Hank's harsh description of Tracy's death. "We need to work up a plan for visitation. To have some kind of schedule so we can plan for our days with Riley."

"I don't have any kind of agreement with you, Walsh. And I don't have to. Not with you or with your mother. How is she, by the way?"

Ty blinked at the swift change in subject. "She's fine."

"Oh?" Hank scratched his chin. "Riley told me she gets tired."

"She has fibromyalgia. She has mostly good days, though."

"Still. A sick woman can't be trusted with an active kid like my Riley. That's not good for either of them."

"My mother loves that little girl and I'm always there when she visits."

Hank took another drink. "I guess that's okay, then. I'm still not obliged to give you any kind of agreement. You have no legal leg to stand on and you know it. No grandparents' rights for your mother, either."

"I know that." Ty had read all the statutes and consulted an attorney to arrive at just that same sad truth. "I'm asking you as Riley's uncle, Hank."

"And why would I let her hang around with you and your friends? That's not good for the kid, either."

"What's wrong with my friends?"

Hank gave a greasy smile. "Let's take that hottie, for instance. I know who she is, you know. That Chapman chick who burned up the tabloids in Europe. Have you seen the pictures, Walsh? My buddy Reggie there pulled them up on his phone. Damn, she's got a smoking body. You hitting that?"

"Don't talk about her like that."

"I sure would," Hank went on. "With that pretty, rosy mouth I bet she could suck a guy for hours."

"Enough," Ty growled. He waited a beat, and then spoke again. "Please, Hank. This is about Riley."

"And this is about the fact that I'm the best thing for that little girl. I'm an upstanding citizen whose damn family founded this city. Your sister was a party girl, and you know it."

"Seems to me you party a lot yourself."

"So what if I do? There isn't a dark splotch against me, Walsh. Not a damn mark. You know that."

"That's because of all your buddies in the courts and city hall."

Hank waved one beefy hand. "Whatever. The fact is I'm the fucking paragon here and you're the one running around with that party girl from Boston."

"She isn't like that."

"Don't matter if she is or she isn't. The press is the press and that girl's rep is pretty remarkable. She got into some crazy shit across the pond. Have you two made a sex tape yet? Damn, I'd pay to see a sex tape with her in it."

Ty flexed his hands and placed them flat on the table. He could feel his pulse pounding in his temples but he held on to his control.

"I know we have no standing in court, Hank. You and Linda are good parents to Riley."

Hank's chest puffed up and he leaned back in his chair. "Yeah, we are. Linda takes good care of the kid. But I have the only say in where and when Riley goes anywhere."

"What do you want?" Ty hated to ask but he was out of

ideas right then. "Tell me what you want in exchange for giving us more time with Riley."

"What do I want? You ain't got anything I want, Walsh. Living out there in Stepford with all the other perfect people. Tamed wild animals, that's what you all are. Pets." His gaze slid over to Cassie again. "Except for that Chapman chick. Even you can't tame that one." He looked back at Ty, leaning closer. "Tell me. Does she like to be tied down? She like it rough?"

Ty came to his feet, sending the chair rocking on its legs behind him. "Just think about what I said. I know you don't have to work with us but we appreciate any time we get with Riley."

Hank looked very proud of himself again. Why wouldn't he? Ty was practically licking his boots.

"Sure, sure," Hank said with a nod. "Just keep your nose clean. I wouldn't want any scandal or gossip to touch my sweet little girl's life."

It nearly killed him to kiss Hank's ass but he had no choice. "No. Of course not."

Hank lumbered to his feet, reaching across to take the other unopened bottle of beer in his big fist. "Thanks for the beer." He winked. "Have a good night."

Cassie, Jake and Claire made their way over to him and Ty

didn't miss it when Hank watched Cassie's ass.

"You okay?" Cassie asked.

"Yeah."

"Any progress?"

"He's going to think about it."

"Well, that's something," Claire said.

Ty grunted his agreement but he knew that Hank saying he'd think about it meant absolutely nothing. And from the expression on Cassie's face, she got that too. Hank wouldn't change his mind about visitation and now he had a bone to pick with Ty about Cassie, of all people. Cassie who was so sweet with Riley and so good for him. She was more than just a party girl from Boston. He knew that even if Hank never would.

Cassie wrapped a hand around his arm. "Do you want to shoot another game?"

He shook his head. "I'm ready to go."

"Will we see you tomorrow at my brother's?" Jake asked.

"I think so," Ty told him. "Rick's burgers are hard to turn down."

Claire hugged Cassie. "See you tomorrow, Cassie."

Cassie squeezed her eyes shut as she returned the embrace. A sudden burst of raucous laughter came from Hank's corner of the bar. Ty lifted his head to find the rednecks ogling both Claire and Cassie as they checked out each other's phones. Hank was bent close to one of his cronies and whatever he said had that guy snickering.

"Let's go," he said to Cassie.

Cassie tilted her head in question, but then she just smiled again and the rest of the place faded from his mind. Hank and his near-refusal to consider coming up with a visitation agreement. The guy's disgusting comments about Cassie. The general noise of the bar and the crack of the balls on the pool tables. There was nothing but Cassie and he felt a warmth bloom in his chest.

This was more than sexual. He'd suspected it for a while now. It was her. Just her. He could fall hard for this girl. If she wasn't so tangled up inside about her family and her past they might turn into something real. Something lasting. But after their talk last night?

He suspected she wouldn't stick around Cypress long enough to give them a chance.

Chapter 18

About a week later, Memorial Day weekend was upon them.
Ty hadn't ended up coming by for burgers at Rick's that Sunday
after his talk with Hank and Cassie tried really hard not to take it
personally. By the time they'd had a chance to catch up it was
Wednesday and they shared what was becoming their usual.
Take-out or pizza out at the tent-cabin and more of the best sex
she'd ever had. There was a wall there, though. He was worried
about visitation with Riley and he'd gone back to being that
strong and silent type of guy.

He still laughed and teased and drove her crazy in the best
ways, though. She couldn't complain. They'd grabbed a couple
lattes at the coffee shop just this morning but, since he hadn't
mentioned any weekend plans, she wasn't counting on another
invitation to take up what little bit of time he had with his niece.
She wasn't going to be that girl. Needing to constantly be the
center of attention with her guy. Her guy. When had she started
to think about him that way? He was, though. She might not do
relationships, she never had anyway, but this thing she had going
with Ty sure felt like one. It wasn't as frightening as she might
have thought before meeting her dimpled hottie.

Cassie had been in Cypress Corners going on a month now

and, while she loved being around family, she still didn't know what she wanted to do with her life. She wasn't a fool. She knew she couldn't stay in this state of limbo forever.

So on Friday afternoon she came home to Rick and Harmony's after another day at the shed with Jake. She'd had a lot of fun showing kids the ins and outs of the courses and instructing them on safety over the past couple of days. Whoever would have thought that she would be able to connect with the little guys? Her very favorite little guy was sitting on the couch, playing with his Legos and watching the big screen.

She put her big bag down on the table in the foyer and walked toward the family room.

"Hey there, Nick."

He turned, his face breaking in a smile. "Hi, Aunt Cassie! Watch the dragons with me?"

"Sure."

"My friend Billy got a new dragon and he brought it for show-and-tell today."

"That sounds pretty cool."

Nick nodded, and then turned back to his show.

"Hi, Cassie," Harmony said from the kitchen.

Her sister-in-law was making something for dinner, and it

smelled fantastic. Cassie headed for the kitchen and leaned on the tall counter. She sniffed the air again. "What's for dinner? It smells yummy."

"Lasagna. It's my mother's recipe."

Cassie smiled, and then stilled. "Your mother's recipe?"

She'd met Harmony's parents once and they were both throwbacks to the hippie era. Sweet as could be but a little too organic/free range/grown-with-love for her to completely understand. She couldn't imagine what would go into that lasagna.

Harmony chuckled as she rinsed her hands in the sink. "I know what you're thinking. No tofu, I promise. The only thing that's a little different about this recipe is that it uses goat cheese instead of ricotta."

"Ooh, goat cheese is delicious. I had some at a farm in Northern Italy once. Sat right in the courtyard with the bleating goats while we ate."

"You went to a farm?"

"I went all over Europe, Harmony. And not just the nightclubs and shops."

"I'd love to go to Europe. I've rarely been out of Florida my whole life."

"Hey, I've been everywhere my whole life and look how I turned out."

"Why do you do that?"

"Do what?"

"Put yourself down. You're you, Cassie. We love you, no matter what made you the way you are."

Cassie couldn't argue, not staring straight into Harmony's genuine gaze. She glanced out the French doors toward the backyard. "And what way am I?

"Gun shy, I'd say. A little hesitant to join in. But sweet and kind and funny."

Yes, she supposed she was gun shy and standoffish, but Harmony hadn't said it like she thought Cassie was a bitch. Not like some of the girls in her circle had said time and again.

Cassie looked back at her sister-in-law. "Really? That's how you see me?"

"I know you don't see it, but having you here has been so nice for Rick. He really missed you."

"I missed him, too. And Jake. I don't want to think about leaving."

"Why would you leave?"

Cassie opened her mouth to give a reason but couldn't come

up with one just then. "I have to figure things out. Maybe if my job works out Jake will let me stay on."

Harmony grinned and Cassie didn't have the heart to burst her happy little bubble. She really didn't think there would ever be a permanent place for her anywhere, especially Cypress Corners.

Harmony snapped her fingers. "Oh, you have mail on the table in the front hall."

"Mail? I don't think I've ever really gotten mail."

Harmony scoffed. "Yeah, right."

"I'm totally serious. I never had an address long enough and who was going to write me anyway?" She walked back into the foyer and picked up the thick white envelope, turning it over to read the return address. "Hmm. It's from my bank up in Boston. I haven't touched that account in years."

"How did you live?" Harmony teased.

"I just used credit cards Bill took out for me. Hey, I'm not proud of it but that was just the way we Chapmans do things. Or did them, anyway."

Cassie opened the envelope and found a bank statement folded inside. It didn't show much of a total but she had just over twelve hundred dollars in the balance. The dates of the deposits were all from this past month and from the Cypress Development Company.

"Rick must have set up my direct deposit," she mused aloud.

"That's Rick. He always thinks of the things that need to be done."

Cassie nodded as she looked at the entries. She'd actually earned this money. She'd worked and gotten paid a wage and had taxes taken out and had her own money.

"It's not much but it's mine," she said.

"What's that?" Harmony asked.

"Nothing." Smiling, Cassie tucked the statement back in the envelope and stuck it in her big bag. She walked back toward the kitchen. "Let me help you make the salad or something."

"I'm not going to say no," Harmony said, waving a hand toward the fridge. "Have at it."

After dinner she sat with Nick and watched some Star Wars Lego thing. This domestic family stuff was really nice and she could get used to the love she felt in this house. And from Jake and Claire, too.

"Okay, I have news," Rick said, his voice tight.

Cassie's nerves tingled and she looked at her big brother. Had the photos resurfaced? Was there more evidence of her stupidity pinging around the atmosphere?

"Spill it, Rick."

He looked evenly at her. "Bill's here."

Cassie's stomach dropped to her toes. "What? When?"

"I told you he was coming, sis."

"Forewarned is forearmed," Harmony put in, coming close to Rick to cuddle in tight. "Promise me we don't have to go to dinner with him."

Cassie could see how much Harmony hated their father. Or at least how much she hated how he treated Rick.

"What does he want?" Cassie asked.

"He wants to sit down with you, me and Jake. Dinner at the Clubhouse and no, Harmony, you don't have to come."

"Thank you, honey." She slowly shook her head. "I'm sorry, but I just don't like being around that negativity. Call me all touchy-feeling like my mom but it's not a good time."

"Imagine what your mother would say about Bill's aura?" Rick said, adding a needed touch of levity.

"I suppose he's calling me home." Cassie folded her arms. "Like some kind of pet. Maybe a Chihuahua."

"I don't think so. He just said he wanted to talk to all three of us."

Harmony stiffened. "Tell me Tiffany isn't here, too?"

Cassie watched Rick's face darken. "He didn't mention her, and he usually does. Like she's an actual part of the family."

"That's something, then," Cassie said.

Tiffany was their father's fourth wife and a total bitch. Not a standoffish, hesitant kind of misunderstood bitch but one who would flirt with her stepsons, deride her stepdaughter and call anyone who was a little bit different a freak.

"Oh, that woman." Harmony waved her hands in a move probably meant to clear the air. "Let's not borrow trouble."

Cassie agreed. "So when is this dinner, dare I ask?"

"Tomorrow night. Around six."

"I don't suppose I could tell him I'm busy?" she asked.

Rick just laughed softly and threw his arm around her. "No way. You've been able to skate out of these dinners for years, Cassie. It's time you join us."

"Misery loves company," Harmony quipped.

Cassie found a smile. "That it does."

***

Saturday morning Ty picked Riley up at Hank's. He'd been worried that the guy would decide to renege but apparently there was a gun show up in Orlando again and Hank was busting a gut

261

to go there. He wanted to ask if Hank made sure to lock up all his firearms but he knew when to shut up. He didn't want to poke the bear.

So today they would have Riley until three o'clock. It wasn't much but they'd make due. It was Memorial Day Weekend and he was looking down the business end of a three-day weekend for once. No tours on Monday. Sales Center and Cypress Institute closed. Only the restaurants, shops and recreation would be open for visitors and residents.

As he drove back into Cypress, Riley chattering on to the Minnie doll he'd brought for her, he saw all the Americana decorations leading up to the town square. The streetlamps were hung with red, white and blue bunting and flags flew from every available space. It was really kind of pretty, but he barely noticed. He was too busy thinking about the week he'd had with hardly any Cassie in it.

Sure, the sex their one night together had blown his mind. Holding her after for as long as he wanted was really good, too. He couldn't help but feel like he was waiting for the other shoe to drop, though. There was an end date to her time in Cypress, even if she hadn't set one. It was like she had one foot out the door.

Hank's words last Saturday night still echoed in his head, too. Ty himself didn't give a shit about whatever had gone down with the tabloids and those racy pictures. Giving into temptation one night he'd googled them and they weren't all that bad. A lot of skin but nothing like some girls got away with in her situation. More stuff did come up about the kind of people she ran around with but he wouldn't guilt her by association. Hank sure as hell would, though. Just how determined was he to use Cassie's so-called reputation against Ty and his mother?

"Lousy piece of—" He bit off the rest of his sentence and threw a smile over his shoulder at Riley. "Hey, sweetie. Want to go to the water fountains today? It's nice and warm outside."

"Ooh, yes! I love the fountains!"

The lakeshore across from Rick and Harmony's neighborhood had the most-developed recreation area. In addition to hiking paths and boat rentals there were fishing docks and playground equipment and a water feature that boasted dancing fountains and kid-friendly squirt stations. It was just right for a kid Riley's age, and Ty got a kick out of it when she squealed and ran around like a demon. It had been some time since he'd taken her to a place like that. St. Cloud had a large water park near Hank's house but Ty hadn't seen her play in the water since September. But now that Ty lived in Cypress and the fountains were right here? He'd take advantage of them. The outing would do his mother a lot of good, too.

She'd been more tired lately, and he knew it was because she was trying to do too much. On days she went into the town center and hung out with Lettie, she was bright and relaxed in the evenings. But the other days, when she spent her time cooped up in the house and cleaning, she looked worn out when he stopped by the house.

"Let's get Grandma to come with us, Riley," Ty said. "What do you think?"

"Yes, yes, yes!"

Laughing, he pulled into the garage and put his mother on the task of getting the little girl dressed in her bathing suit and slathered up with sunblock. He pulled on board shorts and a T-shirt and slid into flip-flops. He knew Riley would need minding and he didn't want his mother to have to worry about chasing her through the water jets.

Armed with beach towels, hats and more sunblock for later, the three of them got out of the Camry and hurried toward the fountains.

"Ty, this was a lovely idea," his mother said, a big smile on her face. "I might just join Riley in the water jets."

"Mom, I would pay to see that," Ty teased.

He found a couple of lounges set beneath a sprawling live oak and set their stuff down. His mother got settled and waved him away.

"I'll watch this stuff, Ty. Go. Take our little sprite into the jets before she bursts."

Riley looked so excited she was practically spinning. "Come on, Uncle Ty!"

He didn't really have to go under the jets with her but he stripped his shirt off and kicked the flip flops under the lounger. "Okay, sweetie. Okay."

The waters were dancing as they made their way onto the large, round rubberized surface. There were several kids running in and out of the vertical pillars of water, yelling and whooping and having a blast. Ty held onto Riley's hand and tugged her toward the smaller bubblers set around the perimeter.

"Look at this one, Riley."

He put his foot over it and the water spread to spray Riley's legs and belly. She laughed and squealed and began to pinwheel her arms as she ran around in small circles.

"That's it." He stepped back, crossing his arms over his

chest. "Go, girl!"

One of the large water pillars chose that second to shoot up right in front of him, soaking him head to toe. He pulled back and bumped into another wet body, this one taller than one of the kids'. Turning, he saw it was Cassie. She grinned up at him. Her hands were on her hips and she was wearing some smoking hot bikini she must have bought in Paris or someplace he'd never been. It was purple and small and clung to every sweet curve on her body.

"Hey, Ty." She tilted her head and her wet ponytail fell over one shoulder. "Great minds."

"Think alike, yeah." He brushed his wet hair back from his face. "It's good to see you."

"I can tell," she teased.

He knew he wasn't giving anything away in his baggy board shorts so he resisted the urge to glance down to make sure.

"Maybe you should come closer," he teased right back.

"Cassie!" Riley yelled with obvious excitement.

"Hey there, pretty girl," Cassie said.

Riley ran off, yelling again when she saw Rick and Harmony's son Nick. The two of them started flapping their arms, looking like flying fish as they dodged and crashed through the water jets and bubblers.

"So how long do you have her today?" Cassie asked.

"Just until three." He watched the two kids a little bit more. "We're making the best of the day, though."

"Nick begged me to take him here and I thought I'd give Rick and Harmony some alone time."

Water shot up again, coming down to course over her skin to pool between her breasts. He struggled to keep his eyes on her beautiful face instead of her ridiculously hot body. It was tough, though.

"So what are you doing for dinner tonight?" he asked. And after, but that was for a later conversation when there weren't so many pairs of little ears in the vicinity.

"Tonight? My brothers and I are having dinner with our father, believe it or not."

She looked confused and worried but before Ty could say any words of encouragement Riley chose that exact moment to grab Cassie around her legs, sending her barreling into him. He caught her tight up against him and she felt so good. Hot skin, cool water, smooth and slick and just right against his chest. The two of them fought to stay upright as they got caught in a water pillar.

Laughing, they clung to each other and he braced his legs apart for better leverage. After staring down into her face he somehow fought the desire to kiss the hell out of her.

He leaned back. "You okay?"

She brushed a strand of wet hair out of her eyes and smiled. "Yeah." Her hand settled over his heart. "Very okay."

He was starting to get hard in his board shorts now and wouldn't that just be fantastic right then? Setting her from him, he took a breath.

"Dinner with your father?"

"Yeah. I have no idea what I'm going to say to him. Or what he's going to say to me, for that matter." Her brows knit. "I'm a big girl. I can do this."

He placed a hand on her shoulder. "Your brothers will be there. They'll have your back. They always do."

She brightened a little. "You noticed that, did you?"

He nodded. "Call me tonight if you need to talk."

"I think I'm going to need to drink, but okay."

The moment stretched until he put a little bit more distance between them. They stepped back, side by side, and watched the kids having a blast. They looked so free and happy. Without a care in the world. He wanted that for once. To just let go and not worry about his mother's health and his niece's well-being. He was learning, though. Trying to take some time just for himself. And what did he want to do with that time?

Spend it with Cassie. For as long as she let him.

Chapter 19

Cassie sat in the passenger seat of Rick's SUV. She'd dressed for the Clubhouse, in a wrap dress of deep burgundy with her hair brushed to one side. She wore black heels and was armed with her favorite studded leather clutch purse. Her heart had been beating double time since she'd gotten ready for this dinner, and she couldn't seem to calm herself. The vehicle rolled swiftly toward the center of Cypress. And their imminent dinner with their father.

"What do you think he's going to do to me?" she asked.

"What makes you think this trip is about you?" Jake asked from the backseat.

"I'm the one he banished here, Jake. I'm the big disappointment."

"This time," Rick said, gripping the wheel. "We've all had our share of horrible dinners with Bill. At least Tiffany won't be there."

"Do you know that for sure?" Jake asked. "I'd like to think we can have a meal without stepmom groping me under the table."

"Eww, she does that?" Cassie asked.

"Yep," her brothers answered at the same time.

She gave a shudder. "I don't know what I'm going to say. Or what he's going to say. What if he sends me up to Boston? Or what if he decides I need to stay here?"

"It sounds like you don't know which scenario would be worse," Rick said.

"I don't," she admitted.

"You better decide, Cass," Jake said. "Bill can't make you do what you don't want to. Whatever that turns out to be."

She blew out a breath. "If you two are going to be rational, I can't have this conversation with you."

Jake leaned forward and tugged on her hair. "Easy, brat. We got this."

She looked back at him, seeing the sincerity stamped on his face. She faced forward again. "Thanks, guys."

"Don't thank us yet," Rick said as they pulled into the Clubhouse parking lot.

"Yeah. You never know how these things are going to go." She sighed. "Wonderful."

Rick parked and the three of them went through the large entrance hall toward the hostess station.

"Good evening, Rick," the hostess said with a smile. She nodded to Jake and Cassie. "Mr. Chapman is already seated.

The hostess escorted them to a table near the wide windows that framed the rolling hills of the golf course beyond. Her brothers bracketed her to the front and back as they headed for their father's table.

"This is weird," Jake said, bending down to Cassie's ear.

"Why?" Cassie asked him.

"Bill usually prefers to be in the center of things," Rick answered. "The guy everyone watches."

If that were true, maybe she had a lot more to worry about than she already was. It wasn't a secluded table but, set as it was a bit apart from the nearby tables, it would give him enough privacy to say whatever the hell he'd come to say tonight.

The candlelight, the clink of glasses, the fine linen tablecloths all spoke of easy luxury Cassie knew was a whole different side of Cypress Corners. And she'd been right. The Clubhouse was just their father's element.

"Hello." Bill came to his feet and Cassie was once more relieved to have on heels. "It's good to see you three together."

Rick and Jake just nodded but Cassie studied her father for a long minute.

"Come give your father a kiss, Cassandra."

She blinked. "Are you kidding?"

Bill actually walked around the table to give her a peck on the cheek. It was so out of the norm that she nearly gawked at him. He smiled at her, actually smiled, and then waved a hand toward the chairs.

"Sit, sit." He looked at the hostess. "Send over the sommelier."

The woman nodded and went to inform the wine steward to come to their table.

"Good," Rick said. "I could sure use a glass or two."

Jake looked down as a smile teased his lips. Cassie sat and put the napkin on her lap out of habit. She'd been in enough fancy restaurants with Bill over the years. That was for sure. In Europe she might have gone drinking and partying in pricey clubs but she rarely ate in formal places. This muscle memory came directly from her dutiful dinners with Bill whenever he summoned her. She blew out a breath. That wine steward couldn't get here fast enough.

"You look good, Cassandra," her father said.

He did, too. Hale and hardy and Chapman all over.

"Thanks, Dad," she said.

"What have you all been doing?" he asked, his gaze bouncing among all three of them.

Rick just met his gaze. "Selling Cypress. I love the place and I'm really good at getting that across to potential residents."

Bill nodded. "Yeah, the investors have been very happy. What about you, Cassandra? I know you weren't happy when I sent you here."

Cassie shrugged. "That's true, but it's growing on me. I've been trying a few things. I'm working with Jake on the adventure courses."

"Really?" Bill gave her a look of approval and she almost fell off her chair. "And what about you, Jake? Staying alive, I see."

"Yep."

Jake's short answer spoke volumes. To everyone's relief, the steward arrived to fill the awkward silence. Wine was discussed and selected and soon poured. Taking up her glass of pinot grigio, Cassie took a long sip.

"I have something to tell you," Bill said after a beat.

She swallowed and carefully set her glass down. "Me?"

"All of you," Bill said.

"I thought this could at least wait until dessert," Jake muttered.

"Tiffany and I are getting a divorce," Bill announced. "It

274

should be final by next month."

Her brothers looked surprised, and then they both narrowed their eyes.

"Let me guess," Rick said. "She's taking you to the cleaners."

"Chapman is bankrupt because she used it as a down payment on a facelift," Jake put in.

Bill shook his head. "She's not getting a penny of Chapman money. She cheated on me, and more than once."

Cassie saw a flicker of real hurt on her father's face. As little as he ever let his emotions show, this was a revelation.

"I'm sorry, Dad," she said.

Bill waved a hand, the vulnerability gone in the next second. "It taught me a lesson, though. You can't keep things hidden. Not forever, anyway."

The server came by just after that cryptic statement and began to list the specials. Her mind still on whatever her father was getting at, she simply chose the salmon and her brothers both picked the porterhouse. Bill ordered the steak too and the waiter left with a promise to bring them a basket of freshly baked bread.

She and her brothers did most of the talking as the meal

continue, though there really wasn't much conversation. The food was excellent and the wine superb but she couldn't shake the feeling that whatever their father planned on spilling after dessert wasn't something any of them would want to hear.

As coffee was poured, Cassie felt the shift in tension at the table. Her brothers didn't seem like they were going to broach any subject with Bill so she took it upon herself to question him. What was the worst he could do? Send her somewhere else?

That fleeting thought gave her pause. She didn't want to leave Cypress Corners. She didn't want to go back to only emailing her brothers and having no one real in her life. She didn't want to leave Ty.

"Dad, I know you have more to tell us than your divorce," she said.

Bill nodded and set his coffee cup aside. "I do, Cassandra. I have something to tell all of you."

"Spill," Jake said.

Bill took a few moments to look each of them in the face, and then spoke. "You have a brother. A half-brother, actually."

Cassie gasped.

"What the hell are you talking about?" Rick asked, keeping his voice low.

"A brother?" Jake asked. "Not with that bitch Tiffany."

Bill shook his head. "No. Tiffany isn't his mother. His mother passed away last winter."

"I don't understand," Cassie said. "Who was she?"

Bill fiddled with a teaspoon as he stared at the table. "She was someone I knew a long time ago. We…had an affair."

Rick cursed softly and ran his hand over his hair. "How old is this brother?"

"Twenty-eight."

"Right between me and Jake." Cassie whispered. "What's his name?"

"Why didn't we know about him?" Jake asked.

Bill held up his hands to hold their questions. "His name is Ben. Ben Chapman."

"So he's your legal son?" Rick asked.

Cassie gave her big brother props for cutting to the chase.

"Your legal son. Our brother," she said. "Yet we've never even heard of him?"

"Did he grow up in Boston, too?" Jake asked.

"No," Bill answered. "He grew up in California. Santa Cruz."

"Does he know about us?" Cassie asked.

"He does now," Bill said. "I spoke to him before I came down here. I've taken care of him all his life but we never had a relationship."

"Sounds familiar," Rick said.

"This is…" Jake shook his head. "I don't even know what this is."

"I'm sorry, kids," Bill said.

"Did Mom know?" Cassie asked.

Bill's gaze slid away from them. "Yes."

His answer was short but it held a huge weight. Their mother knew their father had another child and she never told them?

"I know I was never around for you kids," Bill said. "I know that, and I admit I took the out your mother forced on me."

"Forced on you?" Rick growled. "What the hell are you saying?"

"We were having trouble, your mother and I. I had a fling with my secretary. It wasn't a long affair. Just a couple of weeks. She got pregnant."

"With our brother," Cassie said, still trying to wrap her head around it all.

"I told your mother. We reconciled only after I promised her

I'd never mention it to you kids."

"But you left her in the end," Jake said. "You left her and us."

The expression on Jake's face showed the hurt they'd all felt by Bill's desertion.

"We fought," Bill said. "You have to remember that."

"I remember Mom crying a lot," Cassie said.

Bill's lips thinned. "I wasn't happy, either."

"So you left and basically cut off all contact with us, except for your bank account," Rick said.

"It was the only way your mother would agree to a divorce."

The table fell silent again. Cassie looked at her brothers, and saw the truth dawning on them at the same second she got it.

"She insisted you stay away in exchange for a divorce?" she asked.

Bill nodded. "I took the out she gave me. I'm sorry. I should have been in your lives."

"We're fine without you," Rick said. "Then and now."

"You're not, but you're all adults now. I wanted you to know about Ben and I told him about you, too."

Cassie sat back, feeling like all the air had been sucked out of the room. Her mother had known about their half-brother?

She'd kept that secret and kept their father away from them as punishment?

"I can't believe Mom would do that," Jake said.

"Your mother was a good woman, Jake. But she wasn't a saint."

Jake and Rick sank back in their chairs and they looked as shell-shocked as she felt.

"I'm heading back up to Boston tomorrow," Bill said. "I'll send you Ben's contact info and you three can take it from there."

"Washing your hands again, are you?" Rick asked.

Bill winced. "Not this time. I'm giving you space, Rick. All of you." He smiled at Cassie. "I'm proud of you, Cassandra. It seems you found yourself right where you're supposed to be."

"With my family," she breathed.

Their father nodded and came to his feet. "I've taken care of the bill. Stay here and talk if you like. I'll be in touch."

Bill kissed Cassie's cheek and patted her brothers' shoulders. More touch-feely stuff from him? Taken with the crap they'd just waded through it wasn't that strange.

"I can't believe it," she said after he'd left.

"Which part?" Jake asked.

"All of it. It's a lot to take in."

Jake and Rick each covered her hands and she held on.

"Let's go home," she said. "You two need to see Harmony and Claire and I need... I don't know what I need but I have to get out of this restaurant."

Her brothers exchanged a knowing look, and then Jake lifted his chin. "Text him, sis. We'll wait with you until he picks you up."

With trembling fingers, she sent Ty a text. She had to have something solid to hold onto right now, when the entire world she'd grown up with had just been shaken to its core.

And there was no one more solid than Ty.

***

"Another brother?" Ty asked.

"Yep," Cassie said. "Just a little bit older than I am. And we never knew."

Ty gave her quiet for the moment. Her text had been a surprise tonight. He'd ignored his mother's smug smile as he'd told her he was going to meet Cassie but when he'd seen her and her two brothers he'd known this wasn't a booty call. No. Something had happened. Something big.

She was pale and Rick and Jake were both visibly agitated.

They'd hugged her and she'd clung to them before moving to get in his truck.

"I don't think I ever knew either of my parents, Ty. My mother knew about our half-brother all along and never told us."

"She was hurt."

"You know our father was never really in our lives."

Ty nodded. "That's the impression I got from what Rick and Jake said about him."

She folded her arms. "And now we find out that our mother insisted on that. He was the prick who did what she said, though. Coward."

Ty chose his words carefully. She didn't need him throwing in his opinion about her parents. He could tell her what he believed, though.

"I don't understand all that happened in your family but I can tell you I would never let anybody keep me from my kids."

Cassie shot him a look. "I know. Look at all the crap you put up with from Hank to see Riley."

The silence held until they got to the tent-cabin and went inside. When he unlocked the door she walked in and headed straight on through to the back porch. He followed and found her curled up on a chair with her arms wrapped around her knees.

She'd kicked her shoes off and she looked very vulnerable right then. She'd been hurt tonight, they all had, and he forced himself to take his cue from her going forward.

"What the hell is it with family, anyway?" she asked, leaning her head back.

"Damned if I know." He sat in the other chair. "I've been trying to figure that out for a while now."

She sighed and turned to him. "I'm sorry. I'm going on about having a new brother and you've been dealing with losing your sister all this time."

He shrugged. "It is what it is, Cassie. We move forward and try to make it work."

She smiled, but it was a little sad. "You're a philosopher too?"

He laughed softly. "Nope."

"How do I move forward, Ty? I want to figure this out but I don't know how."

"What do your brothers think?"

"You saw them. They're as freaked out as I am." She pulled her hair back and twisted it somehow to keep it off her neck. "We'll have to talk about it. I'm not looking forward to it, though."

"It can't be worse than my talk with Hank at the End Zone."

"You never told me what he said."

Ty didn't really want to talk about the shit Hank had spewed that night. He owed her the truth, though. Hank had mentioned her specifically.

"He recognized you," he told her.

She bit her lower lip. "From the pictures?"

"Yeah. He was making noise about not letting gossip and scandal around his little girl."

"Oh, Ty. Oh, no. I'd die if anything I did keeps Riley from you!"

"It won't, Cassie. Some pictures from months ago in a tabloid? It doesn't mean anything."

"Still. I'd hate to give him any reason to be an even bigger dick."

He smiled. "Don't worry about Hank. You have enough going on, I think."

To his shock, her face crumbled and she let out a sob. "My mother lied, Ty. She lied about our brother every day she didn't tell us about him. And she lied about our father wanting to stay away."

"Come here."

She unfolded herself and came into his arms, settling on his lap and tucking her face up against his neck.

"Hold me, Ty." Her breath was warm and sweet against his skin. "I need you to hold me."

He cupped her face and brought his brow to hers. "Anything you want, Cassie."

"Anything I want?" She pulled back, her blue eyes so dark at she stared up at him. "I want you."

Chapter 20

"Baby, I couldn't say no to that if I was sitting waist deep in ice water."

His words made her want everything he could give her. And to give him every bit of herself.

Grabbing her to him, he kissed her. She moaned as she took his tongue and he let out a growl. Her body was on fire for him and she was so grateful she was wearing a dress. His quick, sure hands tugged up the skirt, and then he cupped her butt through her skimpiest pair of panties.

She turned to straddle him and he moaned.

"You feel so damn good," he said, kissing her throat.

Her hands got busy, too. She reached under his shirt and her fingernails scraped lightly over his ridged belly before she cupped him. He throbbed against her touch and pulled her closer. Right up against his hard ridge.

He worked himself free of his jeans and when her hand wrapped around him he trembled. She felt the flare of heat that was between them from the first, but there was a tenderness too. A connection. She craved it. She craved him.

"Now, Ty," she said, moving to take him inside.

"Condom," he bit out.

"No time," she whispered.

"Cassie."

"The pill. I'm on the pill. And it's only been you, Ty." She kissed him again. "In such a long time."

"You too, Cassie." He lifted her just enough to slip inside her. "Only you."

His words turned her on as much as his touch. She held on tight to his shoulders and arched, riding him as he moved inside her. It felt so good to have him right there where she needed him. To have him as close as anyone could ever be. Closer than anyone had ever been.

"Cassie, Cassie."

His breathing was harsh in her ear as she held on tighter.

"Oh, my God," she breathed.

She felt it coming, the pleasure that only he ever gave her. It was wild and amazing and she was there for the entire ride. Shaking, she came and cried out his name.

He climaxed then, deep and high inside. Collapsing against him, she breathed in his scent and knew she'd always remember this. It was a melancholy thought after such an explosive experience.

"Ty." She couldn't say anything else. Just his name.

He kissed her so gently as she held him inside her and she thought she could stay there forever. The cool breeze. The chirping of the crickets. The lapping of the water. It was nothing she'd ever felt before. She didn't want it to ever end, but they finally untangled themselves.

"I should get home," she said.

Ty gave her a slow smile, one she'd never seen before. Something had shifted between them. He obviously felt it too but she doubted he could give it a name. She was at a loss. Was this love? Who knew?

"Sure thing."

The next morning she woke, snug in her bed in Rick and Harmony's guest room. The memory of her time with Ty, the talking and the lovemaking, was fresh in her mind. She had to figure this out. This love thing. She'd never felt it before with any other guy. That was for sure. She knew she didn't want to screw it up, though.

A knock came at her door and she rolled over to peer at the screen on her phone. She saw it was after ten and figured the family was up and about. Nick hadn't come barreling into her room this morning, though. Shoving her hair back, she stretched with a yawn and rubbed her eyes.

"Come in." she called.

The door opened and Harmony poked her head inside. She looked worried and Cassie felt a trill of alarm.

"Cassie, I'm sorry to wake you."

"You didn't. Not really." She sat up. "What's wrong?"

Harmony's brow furrowed. "You need to see for yourself."

"Harmony, you're scaring me."

Harmony shook her head. "Just come on, sweetie. Maybe it's not as bad as it looks."

Cassie gaped at her, and then got out of bed and hurried to the door. Rick was seated at the tall counter, bent over his tablet. Her brother wore a dark expression.

"Rick." Cassie came closer, almost afraid to see what had him so angry. "What's wrong?"

He lifted his head and met her gaze. The look in his eyes was a combination of worry and anger. "Sis, you're all over the Internet."

Wrapping her arms around her waist, she took a breath to steel herself. "Show me."

Rick turned the tablet so it faced her, and then clicked. A video began to play, something from TMZ with bursting graphics and crashing music. Photos of her with Wally popped

289

all over the screen while a taunting voiceover filled her ears.

"Cassandra Chapman," the voice said. "Only daughter of multi-millionaire William Chapman and darling of jet-setting partiers, is seen here with the ambassador's son."

"What did Wally do this time?" she wondered aloud.

"Wild Wally, as he's known, has been forced into rehab after his arrest," the voice went on.

"His arrest?" she asked. "For what?"

"Drug dealing and possession." Harmony slid a full cup of coffee in front of Cassie. "He also stole a yacht and hit another boat."

Cassie covered her mouth with her hand, her heart racing. "Tell me no one was killed?"

"Not killed, but hurt pretty badly," Rick said.

The voiceover began again, hitting on some of Wally's best and biggest mistakes accompanied by more pictures and a catchy theme song.

"There's more," Harmony said.

Cassie was angry now. "About me? What the—" She looked around. "Wait. Where's Nick?"

"Watching a movie in our room," Rick said.

Cassie groaned. "It's that bad, then?"

"It's pretty bad, sis."

"Show me."

Rick tapped on another link and a new video began to play.

"Miss Chapman is apparently up to her old tricks again, this time on our side of the pond," the voiceover gleefully declared.

"What are they talking about?" she asked.

Rick shook his head. "Just watch. It sucks."

More pictures filled the screen of the tablet, shots of her in her bikini at the water fountains. The photos must have been taken just the other day, and clearly showed Ty as her companion. The shots were taken so it looked like they were all over each other.

"Wild-child Cassandra retreated to the pricey, picture-perfect hamlet of Cypress Corners, no doubt to get away from her European scandal earlier in the spring."

"I knew I couldn't outrun those pictures." She shakily brought the cup of coffee to her lips and took a sip. "And now they've ruined everything."

"What's ruined?" Harmony asked.

"My life," Cassie said.

"Who is this new boy toy?" the voiceover asked. "He's been identified as Tyler Walsh, a wild animal expert from that same area."

"Oh my God, Ty!" Cassie's eyes filled with tears. "He'll be devastated when he finds out he's plastered all over the place."

"Ty's a big boy," Rick said.

"No, Rick. You don't understand. Riley's father is looking for any reason to screw with Ty's visitation. Just the other night he said he doesn't want any scandal or gossip touching his little girl."

Harmony cursed softly, shocking Cassie. "That man is horrid, keeping that sweet child away from her grandma and uncle."

"He's her father, Harmony." Cassie ran a hand over her face. "This is terrible. If this show is running this story it must be all over the place."

"I Googled it," Rick said, his voice flat. "You hit the nail on the head."

"Oh, no." Cassie sank down on the nearest barstool. "It's over. Everything."

Tinny laughter from the tablet filled the room as the background noise swelled from the tablet. "Maybe he can tame Cassandra's wild ways," a voice put in. "He looks like he's having a damn fine time trying."

"Cassandra isn't the first wild girl in his life," the first voice stated. "His sister was a real party girl who killed herself two years ago."

"No," Cassie rasped. She buried her face in her hands. "Shut it off."

Rick must have done as she asked, because the kitchen was suddenly quiet.

"It'll be okay, Cassie," Harmony said.

Cassie shook her head, swiping at her tears. "It won't be. Don't you see that? Even if Ty doesn't lose any time with Riley no one will want to associate with me down here. I'll be a pariah."

"No. We won't let that happen," Rick said.

"What? My big brothers will swoop in and save the day?" She hopped down off the stool. "Don't you see, Rick? Nothing can save the day. Nothing can save me. I'm a train wreck. I've managed to miss a few of the stops while I've been down here but I won't let my mistakes screw up your lives."

"How will you screw up our lives?" Harmony asked, a determined expression on her face. "You're our family, Cassie. We love you."

"Love isn't enough," Cassie rasped, her throat tight. "My

mess will poison everything that's good down here. Your lives. Your work. Your reputations."

"Cassie, come on," Rick began. "You're taking this too hard."

"You haven't been through this, Rick. Wally fucked up big time but I'm the fool that thought I couldn't be dragged back into the spotlight."

She picked up her coffee and started to head for the stairs.

"Where are you going?" Harmony asked.

"I have to figure this out. I know those pictures look way worse than the situation actually was. That's the way these things go." She pointed toward Rick's now-dark tablet. "Just look how filthy those pictures of me and Ty appear. We were laughing, for God's sake. I remember that moment. Riley grabbed my legs and I felt into him but do you think whoever took that photo cares about the truth? And to mention Ty's poor sister? It's just too much."

"What are you going to do?" Harmony asked.

She started to climb the stairs. "Some thinking, for starters. There's one thing I know for sure."

"I'm almost afraid to ask," Rick said.

"I have to get myself and my mess out of Cypress Corners."

Rick and Harmony said nothing as she retreated to her guest room. Her big brother wouldn't understand. He was used to fixing things but she wasn't his project or his problem. He deserved more. They all deserved more.

Picking up her phone, she opened the browser and with very little searching she found more mentions of Wally's mess in Europe and her own right here at home. The titillation of Ty's sister's tragedy was brought up more frequently with every article she pulled up. This was a shit-storm of monumental proportions and there would be no coming back from it for her.

She had no place to go. No home at all. Not in Boston with Bill. Not here with her family who had opened their hearts to her. She had to put as much distance between herself and all of them for their own good. But worst of all, she had to stay away from Ty.

Flinging her phone onto the floor, she collapsed on the bed and cried.

Chapter 21

"Happy Memorial Day, Ty."

"You too, Mom." His mother looked somber this morning and his stomach clenched. "Are you feeling okay?"

"I'm fine, son. I promise you. I just want you to be prepared."

"Prepared for what?" He dug into the breakfast casserole his mother made and popped his dish in the microwave. "I don't have any plans today."

"That's good. I'm glad Cypress is basically shut down on Memorial Day."

"Why?" The microwave dinged and he set his dish on the tall counter. "What's up?"

She fidgeted in her chair. "Have you talked to Cassie since Saturday night?"

"No." In fact, he'd called her yesterday but she hadn't returned any of his voicemails. "Why?"

"I don't want to gossip. Believe me, son. But this isn't anything like rumors about who fancies whom or who's having a baby. This is big."

His pulse began to trip. "Mom, what are you talking about?"

"One of those news shows got a hold of pictures of Cassie."

"I know about the pictures."

"You do? Do you know what they're saying about you?"

"About me? What do I have to do with those pictures from months ago?"

She sniffed. "Tyler, the pictures are of you and Cassie. From the day you took Riley to the fountains."

He gaped at her. "Are you serious?"

"Check my laptop. I went online to check my email and my homepage was bracketed all over with photos and links to the story."

Ty crossed to the desk set in one corner of the family room and opened the web browser. Blurry close-ups of him and Cassie from Saturday alternated with those old photos of her. They looked bad. Really bad. His mother wasn't wrong, either. Yahoo and Google and just about every site he clicked on was featuring the story.

"This is unbelievable. Cassie must be floored."

"I'm sure. But Ty, there's more."

He turned to see his mother's worried expression again. "What? Tell me."

"They're talking about Tracy."

"Why the hell are they dragging her into this?"

"They figured out your name and found out what happened to Tracy."

"What do you mean?" he asked, his speech deliberate.

"How she lived, Ty." She wiped away a tear. "How she died. They're saying you have experience with party girls."

Ty slammed his fist on the counter. "That's bullshit!"

"I know that," his mother said. She didn't even chide him for cursing, so he knew she was torn up about this too. "What do you think Hank will do?"

"Who gives a shit?"

"He can decide to keep Riley from ever seeing us."

"No." Ty shook his head. "No. He'd never do that. Linda would be worn down to a nub if he didn't find a way to give her a break now and then. Besides, free child care is hard to find."

"That's not what we are, Tyler."

"Aren't we?"

He grabbed his keys and started for the garage.

"Where are you going?"

"To see Cassie. She must be wrecked about this." He stopped at the door and turned back to her. "You're okay with that, Mom? With me and Cassie, that is?"

She smiled through her tears. "She's a sweet girl, Ty.

Nothing these pictures show make a difference to me. Do you love her?"

He was dumbstruck as the truth hit him square in the gut. "I do. I love her."

"Then tell her it'll be okay. Tell her you love her."

"What if that isn't enough?"

She laughed softly. "Oh, it's enough."

He climbed in his truck and headed over to Rick's. The lakeshore recreational area was teeming with folks out for the holiday but he found a place to park not far from the house. He went up the porch steps and knocked on the screen door frame.

The door opened but at first Ty didn't see anybody standing there.

"Hey, Ty!" Nick said, peering up at him.

Ty smiled down at the little boy. "Hey there, Nick. Your Aunt Cassie around?"

"Nope."

"She's not?"

Nick shook his head, and then looked back over his shoulder. "Mommy, Ty's here!"

With that, Nick ran back into the house. Harmony soon stood there in the doorway, her head tilted to one side. "Hi, Ty."

Her voice sounded strained.

"Where is she?" he asked her.

Harmony ushered him inside. "She's gone. She said she had to think."

"Why? Because of those fu—" He stopped himself. "Because of those stories?"

"You didn't see her. She was devastated."

"She's being dragged through the mud," Ty agreed. "It's disgusting, what they're saying. First about her and that Wally guy and now the two of us."

Harmony shook her head. "No. You misunderstand. She's not worried about herself or her own reputation. She's worried about us." She put a hand on his arm. "About you."

Ty raked his fingers through his hair. "So she went back to Boston?"

"Boston?" Rick joined them in the entryway. "Hell no. She wouldn't go back there."

"Then where is she?" he asked him.

"Come on, man. Can't you guess?"

Suddenly the image of her at his tent-cabin came to him. Sitting on his porch. Laying in his bed. Curling up in his arms.

"Thanks."

"Hold it." Rick grabbed his arm. "Are you going to let this shit-storm end things? I know you have a lot at stake."

Ty knew he was talking about Riley. "My niece is very important to me, Rick. But I love your sister."

"You love her?" Harmony clasped her hands, her eyes bright. "I knew it!"

Ty could only nod. "I have go."

"Good. Fix this, Ty." Rick released his hold. "We want her here. With us. But we also want her to be happy."

"Me, too."

Ty left their house and headed out to the far lakeshore. His phone buzzed just as he pulled in and parked. Grabbing it, he got out of the truck and thumbed through to get the message.

Ty, things happened that can't be undone. What we had was fun but fun isn't worth it. Thanks for everything.

He stared at the screen. "Like hell."

He stalked around to the back porch, where she was just as he expected to find her. She stared out at the lake, with a look of resignation on her face. Her mouth was set and her brows drawn together.

"Are you kidding me with this?" he asked, stepping up on the planks and holding his phone toward her.

She jumped a little, and then faced him fully. "It's better this way."

"Yeah?" He shoved his phone in his pocket. "Then why the hell are you out here?"

She glanced away. "I wanted to see it one last time."

"You're not leaving." It was a statement and a question.

She shook her head. "Cypress? No."

His heart thudded to a stop. "You're leaving me."

At her slow nod he squeezed his eyes shut. "Cassie, don't do this. What we have… This isn't just fun."

"I had fun. I thought you did, too."

He opened his eyes and blew out a breath. "Damn it, that's not what I mean."

"Then tell me what you mean? Because as I see it, I screwed up again and more people than just me are going to pay for it."

"It's just a few pictures."

"They talked about your sister, Ty. They made her sound like a mess and that you're used to cleaning up messes. Like me."

Ty came close to her, sitting down at her feet. "Cassie, she was a mess. You're not."

She looked out toward the lake again, her gaze filled with

sadness. "I brought this on myself, Ty. I have to try to fix it but most importantly I have to keep the damage to a minimum. That means staying away from you."

"I won't let you."

She looked at him, her lips parted in surprise. "You won't let me? Listen, nature boy. I'm not some wild animal you have to tame. I know you couldn't save your sister. I know that eats you up inside. But you don't have to save me."

The truth was inside of him and he'd faced it already. Now he had to let her know without screwing everything up.

"I don't want to save you," he said.

"What?"

"You don't need saving and I don't want to save you. I want to love you."

***

Cassie stared at Ty's beautiful face. He looked so serious, his hazel eyes intent. He wanted to love her?

"Ty, what are you saying?"

"I love you, Cassie. The rest of it doesn't matter."

"But it does." She felt the tears starting again, just when she thought she'd cried them all out yesterday. "Those pictures. The stories. It can ruin everything."

303

"What, exactly, can it ruin? Hank is a prick. He's never made seeing Riley easy so I don't see how things will be any different."

"He already told you he doesn't want any scandal around Riley. And this is a shit-ton more than just a little bit of it."

Ty quirked a half-smile at her. "He might make a fuss but he likes having his free time." He winked. "And free childcare."

She studied him closely for a minute. "You're serious? You don't care?"

"Oh, I care." He came closer, coming up on his haunches. "I care about what this will do to you."

"Nothing. I don't matter. I'm just worried about my family."

"Don't say that."

"I am worried, Ty. They don't deserve this after all they've done for me."

"I know that, and it tells me just how big your heart is. I meant don't say you don't matter. You matter to them and you sure as hell matter to me."

Her lips began to quiver and she didn't know why she wanted to cry now. This man, this wonderful, almost too-good-to-be-true guy was here telling her just what she needed to hear.

"You mean that."

"I don't lie, Cassie." He smiled again. "Boy scout, remember?"

"And you want to love me?" she had to know.

"Hell, sweetheart. I already love you."

That did it. Tears burst forth and she took in great shuddering breaths as she tried to stop them.

"Holy shit." Ty wrapped his arms around her. "What did I say? I'm sorry."

She sucked in a breath, shaking her head. "Don't you dare apologize. I love you, too."

He put a finger under her chin and lifted her face to his. "Marry me. I know you're staying here in Cypress, Cassie. I need to know you're staying here with me."

She bit her lip, and then wrapped her arms around his neck. "Yes, Ty. I'll stay here with you. I'll marry you, even if you're too good for me."

"Ah, baby. I'm not too good for you." He lifted her in his arms and carried her inside the tent-cabin. "I'm just good."

Laughing, she tumbled with him onto the bed and showed him just how good they could be. Together.

Epilogue

Cassie worked the tangles out of a harness and set the webbed straps down on the counter. The day was winding down and she was tired in a good way. The coming weekend was going to be a pain, though.

In the two month's since she'd accepted Ty's proposal, Harmony and Claire had taken to poring over wedding magazines and going on and on about flowers and cakes and dresses. Harmony knew the language of flowers, of course. And their Latin names. Claire was the baker in the family so she had very particular opinions on tastes and colors for the cake. As for herself? She couldn't care less about any of it. The wedding was set for September and that meant a lot more planning was in her future.

Things were still weird with her father, but she and her brothers had made some contact with their half-brother Ben. He was going to come down for a visit sometime in the summer and she insisted he think about coming down for the wedding. He was working at Chapman in Boston, of all places. She couldn't imagine Bill forging a relationship with him, since they'd learned Ben had as much actual contact with the man growing up as they'd had.

As for the sensational stories about her and Ty? It turned out they were just the flavor of the week and she could almost kiss a certain bad-boy pop star for doing something stupid five days later that filled the tabloids and newsfeeds everywhere. Hank still tried to use it to hold over Ty's head but her guy was so resilient, so steady, that he never let Hank see him sweat.

"Hey there."

She looked up to see Ty standing in the doorway. "Hey, Ty."

He came close and gave her the sweetest kiss. It was hot and promised what she knew they'd share out at the tent-cabin tonight.

"Do we have Riley tomorrow?" she asked.

Ty grinned, his dimples showing. "Yep. Hank was trying to be a prick but apparently he wants to go to the rodeo. Linda insists on going with him, so he's stuck."

"Hmm. I think I'm starting to like Linda."

"She's a good woman. Just beaten down a little around the edges."

Cassie nodded. "What about you?"

"What about me?"

"Are you beaten down around the edges, nature boy?"

He wrapped those strong arms of his around her. "I'm ready and raring to go."

She just bet he was. "Yeah?"

"Yeah. How about we hit that wall?"

Rolling her eyes, she groaned. "If I have to."

"I'm thinking you do."

He'd managed to get her to move her butt more than she ever had over the past few weeks. The climbing walls continued to challenge her and she even went running with him. He could wear her out in the best ways so she figured she needed to keep up her stamina.

Jake popped his head in just then. "You guys go climb. I'll lock up."

"Thanks, Jake," she said.

She walked past her brother, who hip-checked her as she passed him. In return she punched him in the arm and earned a bark of a laugh.

As she climbed up the wall, slowly and carefully, she could see Ty down on the sandy ground holding her rope with his belay device. She didn't need to look to know he was there, though. He would always be there. He proved that time again. He'd keep her safe. He loved her. And she loved him more than she ever thought she could.

Since coming to Cypress Corners she'd learned to love herself, too. She was finally home.

About the Author

JoMarie DeGioia is a bestselling author of Historical and Contemporary Romance. She's known Mickey Mouse from the "inside," has been a copyeditor for her tiny town's newspaper, and a bookseller. A hybrid author, she also writes Young Adult Fantasy/Adventure stories, New Adult Romance and Paranormal Romance. She gets lost in DIY projects around the house and works out plot ideas during long runs. She divides her time between Central Florida and New England.

Discover books by JoMarie DeGioia

The Dashing Nobles series, including

More Than Passion—#1 Historical Romance

Pride and Fire

Just Perfect

More Than Charming—#1 Regency Romance

The Cypress Corners series, including

Finding Harmony

Taming Jake

Loving Cassie

The Gifted YA Fantasy/Adventure Trilogy, including Gifted

The Braunachs of the Dell series, including Luke's Gold

Connect with me online

Twitter: https://twitter.com/JoMarieDeGioia

Facebook: www.facebook.com/JoMarie.DeGioia.Author

Website: www.jomariedegioia.com

www.ingramcontent.com/pod-product-compliance
Lightning Source LLC
Chambersburg PA
CBHW051410170626
46809CB00006B/2101